THE MONSTER IN ME

by Mette Ivie Harrison

Holiday House / New York

Library of Congress Cataloging-in-Publication Data
Harrison, Mette Ivie, 1970–
The monster in me / by Mette Ivie Harrison.—1st ed.
p. cm.
Summary: In a small town near Salt Lake City, Utah, a caring foster family
and her love of running help thirteen-year-old Natalie Wills feel that she can
be part of normal life, despite having been raised by a drug-addicted mother.
ISBN 0–8234–1713–1
[1. Foster home care—Fiction. 2. Family problems—Fiction.
3. Running—Fiction. 4. Interpersonal relations—Fiction. 5. Drug abuse—Fiction.
6. Utah—Fiction.] I. Title.
PZ7.H25612 Mo 2003
[Fic]—dc21   2002069079

DuBOIS

Acknowledgments

Thanks to Rick and Ann, who got me started,

to Carol, who gave me hope,

to Cheri, for laughter,

to Kevin, for friendship,

to Kim, for fun,

and to John, who taught that mistakes

are only possibilities

prologue

I'm lying flat with my arms and legs strapped to the corners of a large metal table. There are vials and tubes everywhere, and it's dark, with mist covering the floor. I'm in Frankenstein's laboratory—like in the movies. And I'm the monster. I'm the creature Dr. Frankenstein has made, the creature who wants desperately to be human, but isn't.

Cramps start in my arms and legs, but all I can do is shiver under the straps. I can't move an inch. When will someone come for me?

I wait and wait. Then I wonder, What if I'm the mistake, the monster that didn't work? What if Dr. Frankenstein isn't coming back?

"Help me!" I try to yell. But no words come out of my mouth. Did the doctor forget to give me a voice?

What else did he forget to give me? I lift my head to look down at my body. Two legs. Two arms. Fingers and toes. It's all there as far as I can see. But what about inside?

I hold my breath and listen for the slightest sound. But there is nothing. No one. How long before I die of thirst? Or starvation?

But I am only a monster. I don't need to eat. I don't need to drink. I don't need to speak. I will live forever, strapped on this table. Alone.

I pull at the bands frantically, trying to get free. I wonder if I can rip my hands off and pull the stumps through, but the doctor has sewn them on too tightly. They aren't human hands, made of flesh and blood. They're made of rubber and steel, and I'm not strong enough to tear them apart.

After a long while, I give up and lie back again on the table. I close my eyes and tell myself that it doesn't matter. I can learn to live this way. I have to.

chapter
one

I wake up late the next morning and make myself get up and dressed. My tongue is coated so thick that I can't talk to anyone I see in the halls. It doesn't matter. Talking's not important right now.

First things first. I have to get out. I rub at my arms, reminding myself that the straps were only part of the dream. They're not real. Still, I can't bear to lace my sneakers up tightly. I leave them loose and tuck the ties in the sides. Then I push open the door of the home, take a breath of city air, and run.

It is a wonderful feeling, running. I'm no rubber and steel monster out here. The blood rushes through my veins, and my feet throb by the time I am finished, the skin raw and fragile. Human.

When I finally come back to the home, I sprawl out on the couch in the living room and wave my arms back and forth to make some wind. Every little movement makes me ache, but even the pain feels good. It means I'm alive.

In a few minutes, Ace and T.K. come in and turn on the television.

I pull myself up so there's room for them on the couch, but they sit on the floor instead. I don't blame them. What's the point in getting to know me? I'm temporary. They're temporary.

I sit there, watching the show, trying not to think about my dream.

About being a monster.

I'm trying so hard not to think that I start at the sound of the front doorbell. Someone else goes to get it and I hear Ms. Beck's voice asking for me.

"Morning, Natalie." Ms. Beck comes over and sits down on the other end of the couch. "How are you today?" she asks, with that look of hers. The one that makes you feel like you're under a microscope and she's counting strands of DNA.

"Fine," I say. I stare at the wall just beyond her head, splattered with ink from some fight years ago.

"Really?"

I shrug. She should spend less time thinking about me and my problems and more time thinking about herself. She could use some self-improvement.

She has the worst taste in clothes I've ever seen. And hers are expensive, so she doesn't even have the thrift store excuse. She wears these black and gray suits that make her into a box. Also, she keeps her hair up in a tight bun that makes her look sixty years old when you can tell from her skin she isn't.

"Why don't you come out into the waiting room?"

4

Ms. Beck asks. "I have some people I'd like you to meet."

My stomach goes cold and hard, like steel and rubber. Like a monster's stomach.

"Natalie?" she asks.

"I told you I'm fine. I don't need to meet anyone."

"And I told you that you don't always know what you need at your age."

I stare her up and down. I don't think she knows what she needs at her age, either.

She smoothes down her skirt and tucks a stray piece of hair behind her ear.

"It might not be as bad as you think," she says.

Or it might, I think. But I stand up.

I walk with her away from the buzzing noise of the television.

Ms. Beck opens the door to the waiting room and waves for me to go first.

I go. Slowly.

The space is small and dingy, with an old brown velvet couch in the corner. Sitting on it is a plump woman with a soft, generous face. It could be worse.

Ms. Beck says something, but I don't catch it. Probably an introduction.

I nod stiffly to the woman.

She smiles at me. "Hello, Natalie."

Ms. Beck turns to the man standing to the side of the couch. "Natalie, this is Mr. Parker."

Foster parents.

"Mr. Parker," I say. He is tall and thin. His fingers are thumping on the wall next to him and his feet are tapping the floor.

"I hear you are a runner," says Mr. Parker. A big smile splits his face.

His teeth are crooked. That makes me feel better. He isn't perfect, either.

"Yeah," I say. "I run."

"Good. I run, too, five or ten miles most days. How about you?"

"Maybe," I say. I don't really keep track. I usually run for an hour or more.

His smile gets tighter. More fake. "Well, I thought we'd run together some time. It'll be a chance for us to talk. You like mornings?"

Now it is my turn to smile. "I'm a night person, Mr. Parker," I say.

But he doesn't look upset at all.

"Call me John," he says. Then he turns to his wife. "John and Alice."

Ms. Beck fidgets. As far as I know, she has no first name.

"Okay, John," I say.

"Good. Now, the first thing that we need to take care of is"—his eyes drift to my feet—"a new pair of shoes."

I pull my toes in from the holes in the seams of my shoes. They haven't lasted too well, but what do you expect? They're secondhand, and I've been running a lot lately.

"I like my shoes," I say.

John's eyebrows rise, but he doesn't argue.

"Well," says Ms. Beck, "I think it's time for you to go get your things now."

I head out, relieved to escape. I go down the hall, third door to the right. I share the room with two other girls, and there's a fourth bed, empty for now.

Lisa is on her bed when I come in, but she doesn't look up from her book the whole time I am pushing shirts from the closet into my duffel bag. I have one pair of cords in the dresser, and stuff them in last.

"You going?" Lisa asks finally, her voice muffled by the book so close to her mouth.

"Yeah," I say. "My big chance." My lips twist.

"Huh," says Lisa. She knows what I mean. "Well, good luck."

"It won't be that long. I'll probably be back before the end of the week."

"Sure." She looks back at her book.

I throw the bag over my shoulder and then, a step past the door, I turn back. "Hey, tell Sharon I said good-bye, all right?" I wish Sharon were here to say good-bye to, since she was the first one to say hello. But who's Sharon to me or me to her, right?

"Okay." Lisa keeps her eyes on her book.

I make my way back to the waiting room. I set the

duffel down at the door and catch the tail end of something Alice is saying.

". . . adopted when I was young and always felt like I ought to give something back."

Oh, brother. Couldn't she just give money? It would be a lot simpler that way.

Ms. Beck looks up and sees me. "Natalie, are you ready so soon?"

"Ready as I'll ever be," I say.

Alice suddenly leans in and gives me a long, squishy hug. I am drowning in the ocean of her perfume.

Better than sweat and vomit, though.

"Maybe you should let her go before you smother her," John says.

Alice tenses and immediately lets go. "Sorry," she says, looking at John more than me.

"It's all right," I mutter.

John reaches for my duffel then, but I don't let go, even when he tugs on it. It is mine—all I have. He finally leaves it in my hands.

"I'll be by tomorrow to see how you're doing, Natalie," Ms. Beck says.

"Great," I say. "Just great."

I should have stayed asleep, in my dream. Being a monster isn't all bad. Compared to being a foster daughter, at least.

chapter two

The Parkers' white sedan is big and clean, looks brand-new. It isn't locked. Crazy, I think. John has to be crazy not to lock this.

"Where would you like to sit?" asks Alice from behind me. Her hand settles on my shoulder. I keep still, unsure how to shake her off.

"Uh—"

"There's room for all of us in the front, if you'd like. Or—"

I pull up on the back door handle and slide myself in.

"You sure you want to be back there?" asks Alice as I close the door.

"She's sure, Alice," says John. "Give her some space, why don't you?"

I am too relieved to feel sorry for Alice. The drive is quiet and relaxing. Then just before we turn off onto I-80, John asks, "You need anything before we're out of gas stations? A drink?"

My throat does feel dry. "A Coke?" I ask.

John pulls off at the next exit. Alice excuses herself to find the rest room while he fills up the car with gas.

"Get whatever you want," he says, handing me a crisp twenty-dollar bill.

It's paper, but it feels heavy in my hand. I've never had that much money before. Even at the group home we worked for privileges, not cash.

"Something wrong?" John asks.

"No, no." I head in to the minimart to look around. I pick out my Coke. Seventy-five cents. It seems a shame to break a twenty for that, but I don't have any choice.

The man at the counter counts out my change. More than nineteen dollars left. I could live a long time on nineteen dollars.

I stuff all the coins and bills into my front pocket, then push through the glass door and watch John clean the windshields as I sip at the Coke fizz. I am thirsty enough to drink it all at once, but I recap it to save the rest for later.

Just in case.

Then I climb into the backseat.

"You get what you need?" John asks, poking his head in the driver-side window.

I nod. I put my hand to my pocket, feeling the bills.

Why doesn't John ask for it? Could it be a test?

I think of T.K. He went to foster parents for a

couple weeks, but he got sent back for stealing. The foster parents didn't file charges against him or anything, but he had to go do community service stuff every weekend instead of going on field trips with the rest of us.

I dig out the change.

"Oh. Thanks." John takes the wad and dumps it on the dashboard without even looking at it.

So it wasn't a test, after all. Too bad I didn't keep it.

John pulls away from the gas tank and lets the car idle until Alice reappears. Her hair is newly fluffed and she's redone her lipstick. She jiggles toward the car.

"Better?" she asks John. I tense up, thinking he'll put her down again.

"The best," he says instead. Alice blushes and gets in.

When we get back on the freeway, it turns east, up into the burnt orange mountains. Now Alice starts asking questions. "How long have you been in the group home?"

"Two months."

"So what do you think of it?"

"It's fine."

"Are you going to miss anyone?"

Instead of answering, I look into the deep green pines cut off at the tree line.

"Alice," says John.

She sighs and goes quiet.

John keeps driving, one hand on the wheel. He is so tall that his head brushes the top of the car even when he is sitting down.

I can't tell where we're going, except that it is through the mountains. I've never been this far away from the city before.

Memories flash in my head. Lisa's crying face when she found out her mom was dead. Sharon's dog-eared picture of the little sister who got to live with her dad. Ace and T.K.'s fistfight that ended in a backyard water fight.

Why am I thinking about them? I was there for two months. So what? Leave it all behind.

After about an hour of steady driving, we come around a bend.

"Almost there," says Alice.

Almost where? I can't see much. A few old, weathered barns and some cows and horses. A farm equipment store that looks like it sells stuff newer than anyone around here ever uses.

A couple blocks farther and I see a row of a few stores that were probably built a hundred and fifty years ago. One says King's. There is a Mercantile Company after that. John slows down at a stoplight near a house with cutesy decorations on the wooden shutters.

It feels like I am in another country, a long time ago. This isn't like Salt Lake City at all.

"The high school is up the road a bit," says Alice.

"What's that?" I point to a row of small, old-fashioned houses.

"The historic Heber village buildings are there, across from the Heber Creeper railroad. Have you heard of it?"

"Heber Creeper?" It sounds like an insect.

"It's fun. Maybe we'll take you on it sometime," says Alice.

"Can't wait," I lie.

John turns off the main road. Then he winds through a few more turns, and pulls into the driveway in front of a light-colored brick house.

The house is so big, so permanent.

My legs start to shake. Probably from too much running this morning.

"Home at last," says Alice as she opens the door.

chapter
three

Alice hurries inside, saying something about lunch.

I look up at the mountains, so close and so real, behind the house. Overwhelming.

"Come on in," says John.

I follow him up the steps and through the doorway.

Then we are in a foyer tiled in black and white. There's a living room off it with thick-piled cream carpet. Everything's a lot nicer than the stuff they had in the group home. It's also a lot messier. There's a sweater on the arm of one of the recliners and socks tucked underneath the couch. There are shoes in a pile by the door, too. Two of them are a new pair of running shoes in a size that could only be John's.

"Lunch in the kitchen, I think," says John.

My stomach grumbles just then, but I can hold out longer.

Still, if they're offering, no reason not to say yes.

John leads me to the kitchen, where Alice is making some sandwiches at the table.

If the food here is good, maybe I'll think about staying. Otherwise it's hardly worth unpacking my duffel. Except that there isn't much in it to begin with.

The sandwich bread is homemade, but it tastes funny to me, and it is so crumbly I have to keep taking bigger and bigger bites. But at least there's no peanut butter. I hate peanut butter.

"Well, I've got to get back to work," says John, swallowing hard on his last big bite of sandwich.

Alice gives him a kiss. Then they both look at me.

They're not going to kiss me, are they?

"See you tonight," says John.

"Yeah, see you." I thought I would be glad to see him go, but he's leaving me alone with Alice. And she's the one with the touchy-feely complex.

Sitting across the table from me, she says, "So?"

Hey, that's supposed to be my line, I think.

A long, uncomfortable silence stretches out. At least she's keeping her distance, even without John around.

"Well, the girls should be home soon," she says after a moment. "Liz is seventeen, a junior. Kate is fourteen, a freshman, and just a few months older than you."

I file away the names. I'm getting good at learning names. And forgetting them, too.

Alice stands up. "Would you like to see your room?" she asks.

"Yes." I pick up my duffel and follow her. Her hips sway from side to side, like the pendulum of a big clock. Tick, tock, tick, tock.

"Here it is." Alice opens the door, then steps aside, letting me go in first.

My first thought is: Only one bed.

My second thought is: Only one bed.

"You can stay in here and unpack or come out and watch television, whichever you prefer."

I look at the deflating duffel on the floor. It won't take me long to unpack.

"Television, please."

Alice shows me the way to the TV, turns it on, and stands to the side. What does she want?

"Thanks," I say.

Her lips twitch, ready to say more. But in the end, she just leaves.

I think how wonderful it is to be alone again. Then I find the remote and turn up the volume as high as I can stand it. My ears throb, but the sensation there makes me numb everywhere else.

Numb is good.

I don't even notice when someone comes in, not until she takes the remote from the couch and changes the channel. She has to be either Kate or Liz, but I don't know which. She has glossy black hair like John's underneath his gray, but her figure is like Alice's.

She stands with her back to me, right in front of the television, blocking my view.

"Uh—excuse me," I say quietly.

She turns and glares at me. "Yeah?"

What do I do? I've been ignored plenty, but no one has ever been so outright obnoxious to me.

Another girl comes in then. This one looks like a miniature version of Alice, blond hair and all. She plops onto the couch next to me. Her thigh touches mine, like we are on a date together.

"Kate, do you mind?" she says, pushing her sister to one side.

So if Kate is the rude one, she must be Liz.

Liz gives me a lopsided smile. "I'm sorry. You'll have to forgive Kate. She's still in preschool, socially."

Kate kicks Liz in the legs. "And you're still playing teacher," she says.

"Hey, someone has to," says Liz. She turns to me. "Well, that's a nice introduction to our family, isn't it?" She puts out a hand. "I'm Liz," she says. "You must be Natalie."

I nod and try to scoot away from her, but the couch is too soft. I keep sliding back toward her.

Kate finally deigns to speak to me. "I'm the actress." She gives me her hand like she's a princess meeting the queen. Then she bows her head, flutters her eyes, and makes a curtsy so deep I'm sure she will fall down.

In fact, she does, and then she slams her fist into the carpet and swears under her breath.

Liz giggles. "You'll have to get used to her doing that kind of thing," she says, waving at Kate on the floor. "She can't help it. Think of it as a disease. Only don't worry. I'm sure it's not contagious."

Liz takes the remote and turns the television to yet another channel. "You think you could move your little sideshow out of our way, Kate?" she asks.

Kate stands up and bares a perfect set of white teeth. Then she sits down on the arm of the couch right next to me. Body snatchers on either side of me. Don't they have any concept of personal space?

I jump up.

"Hey! What's wrong?" asks Liz.

"Nothing," I say. "Nothing." I back away slowly, just to make sure they don't make any sudden movements and trap me again.

"Where are you going?" Liz asks.

"Uh—" I say. "My room." Then I scurry away as fast as I can.

Behind me I hear Liz and Kate arguing. "She hasn't even been here one day, Kate, and already you've scared her away."

"Me?" Kate throws back. "You're the one who mentioned contagious diseases."

I stop in the bathroom on my way to my room. The toilet paper is quilted with little pictures. I feel like

I'm wiping myself with a silk scarf. Maybe I'll get used to it, after a while.

When I come back out, I can hear Kate and Liz still snapping at each other. Sisters, I think. Would Kate and Liz hang on to pictures of each other like Sharon did when everything else in her life had fallen apart?

I go into my room and close the door behind me. Sitting on the bed, I think about home—my real home. Mom was hardly ever there. Which is probably why silence is the only thing that ever really feels like home to me.

chapter
four

I'm back in the lab, but I can hear someone coming. I feel a panicky excitement. I'll be free now. The doctor will set me free.

But when the door creaks open, it's my mom. She's the doctor.

"My monster—" She stares down at me with a wide smile. "Alive." She cackles and leans down to kiss me.

I buck. The strap on my right arm loosens. I strain with all my might, and it snaps. I push Mom into a shelf of vials and they fall on the floor with her, sounding like tinkling bells.

I open the door to the lab and look down the stairs. I have to escape.

But I hesitate for just a moment.

Then I launch myself forward at a run. On the first step, I trip and fall headlong down the whole flight. Mom's voice cries for me as I fall, but I still don't have a voice, so I can't cry out for myself.

I wake up before the crush of landing, but the disoriented feeling of falling remains. Where am I?

I sit up and let my eyes get used to the dark. Gradually, they sort the edges out. A four-drawer dresser to the left of me. A window past that with an inch of pale moonlight shining through it. A double-doored closet in front of the bed. A door to my right, half open, leading to the hallway.

It takes me that long to remember. Ms. Beck at the group home. John and Alice Parker. Heber, Utah. Kate and Liz.

I slip back down into the bed and pull the covers up to my chin. The quilt is thick and stiff, probably never used. Still, I shiver a few times before I settle down. The temperature or the dream? Maybe both.

But the dream is the reason I don't even try to close my eyes and go back to sleep. Even if I could, it would just come back to me. My mind gets caught in a loop sometimes, like a broken movie projector playing the same part over and over again. And for me, it's always the bad part.

What do Kate and Liz dream about? Probably bunnies and fields of flowers.

I wish I could dream about flowers instead of monsters like me.

chapter five

I never do go back to sleep. I lie in bed waiting to hear some sounds of life in the house. Someone other than me awake.

Finally, an alarm goes off. It's still dark outside my window, and the clock says 5:00, but I'm just glad to get away from the dream. I follow the rustling sounds down the hallway, past the kitchen, and into the foyer by the front door.

John's there, bent like a paper clip, stretching his legs. He has on the running shoes I saw by the door before and a crumpled white T-shirt and blue shorts. He pulls himself up when he sees me.

"Natalie. Good. I was worried you wouldn't be coming with me."

Whoops. I forgot about his wanting a running partner.

"Kate and Liz sleep in every morning, so I can't take them."

Lucky Kate and Liz. Smart Kate and Liz.

"But since you're up, there's no reason for you not to come, is there?" asks John.

How to respond to that? If I tell him I usually sleep in, except when I have a bad dream, I might as well invite him to jump inside my brain and take a good look around. I'd rather run ten miles with him.

Tomorrow I'll stay in my room, dream or no dream.

"Why don't you go get something on for running?" says John, pointing at my nightshirt and bare feet.

One last chance to get away. "Are you sure you want to wait for me? I mean, I don't want to mess up your routine." Maybe he likes to be alone as much as I do.

Apparently not.

"No problem," says John. "I'll just do a few extra stretches while I wait. More stretching never hurt anyone." And he bends down into the paper clip again.

The dream hits me again when I open the door to my room. I'm walking stiff, like the monster would. And the fear is in my throat, the feeling of falling, and not knowing where I will land.

I poke through my duffel. Not much to choose from. I have to save my cords for school, which leaves only my jeans from yesterday. At least they don't smell too bad, and I have a clean T-shirt to wear. The only socks I can spare have holes in them, but I figure they'll match my shoes.

When I go back to the foyer the door is open and

John is out on the steps, doing a mini-jog in place. I can see the start of sunshine inching in from the east. The air tastes like cold, fresh water.

"All right," I say. "Let's go."

And I go.

John catches me by the back of the shirt and pulls me back.

I have to grit my teeth to keep from yanking away. "What?"

"You need to warm up first," he says mildly.

Yeah, and who does he think he is? The god of running? I remember him scolding Alice yesterday, and feel a new sympathy for her. "I never warm up," I say. "I don't need to."

"Everyone needs to warm up," says John.

Next he'll be telling me how to brush my teeth and cut my nails.

John just leans against the garage door and waits.

"Fine," I say, finally. I bend down quickly to reach my toes. I do a couple of half jogs. "There, I'm warmed up now. Can we go?"

"No. Do it like this," says John. He turns around and stretches one leg to the bottom step, then leans forward. Then he switches legs.

"Now this." He lifts one arm over his shoulder and pushes it down with the other. "Go on. Try it. I'll bet you'll like it."

Have you heard the word *arrogant*? It was made for John.

But as I set my legs on the right steps, I feel the muscles along the back of my calves start to burn. Hmm. I never knew that's why they call it a warm-up.

I do the arm thing, too. It feels good, actually. Maybe I'll do it next time, when I go out by myself. If I feel like it.

John makes a strange sound, kind of like "Huuup." And he starts off down the driveway, his legs kicking behind him.

I've never run with anyone else before, but I'm glad to see that he isn't going to slow me down. If anything, I'm going to have a tough time keeping up with him. He really does run. None of that jogging thing. This is fast-and-furious-go-someplace-hurt-yourself-running.

Still, it takes me only two or three blocks to fall into the beat. My feet find John's rhythm and the pounding feels good. The air is different here. The roads are different. Everything is different.

Good different.

We go maybe half a mile, pass a gas station, turn west. There aren't many houses even at the beginning of our route, but the farther out we get, the fewer we see. And even those seem more like barns than houses.

Then for a long ten-minute stretch there is nothing but brush and a couple of cows behind a wooden fence. And I'm still going strong.

Until we hit the hill. I close my eyes at first and try to keep up the rhythm. My ears tingle with the cold and my lungs are hot and heavy. The air seems thicker with every step, and I'm panting and wheezing.

I lift my head just long enough to see John at the top. He turns, jogs in place, and waits for me. I drop my head and give everything I have into making the rise. I'm sure I am going to collapse at the top. But something happens there, when the road evens out.

I get my second wind and feel the surge of adrenaline as a smile spreads across my face. Suddenly, I feel like I can go on forever like this.

John wipes the sweat off his forehead, pushing his hair back. His legs keep moving, but not as high as mine.

"You're a natural, you know." He gets it out between breaths.

I laugh once, short and hard, like Mom.

"You ever think of joining a team?"

I turn away. "No," I say.

"You should. Really," he insists.

I make a low sound in my throat and shake my head, keeping my legs moving all the while.

"Hey, Natalie. What did I say?"

"Nothing. I just don't want to join a team, that's all."

"Why not? It would be great for you. I was in cross-country when I was in high school and it was one of the best things I ever did. Taught me discipline and trained me how to meet a challenge. I also found a couple of lifetime friends there. One of them coaches cross-country and track at the high school. Coach Landers."

"Uh-huh," I say.

"Come on, I could introduce you to him, let you see him up close. Then you could decide from there. All right?"

I raise my eyes for just a moment and give him my best freeze. "I don't want to."

John mutters to himself.

The sweat on my back starts to cool, and I shiver. I wait.

"Let's head back then," says John.

I get a head start, keeping up the same pace. But downhill is a lot easier than up. On foot, that is.

I remember the time I borrowed a pair of roller skates from a neighbor. She said downhill was the only way to try them out. I screamed for Mom the whole way. I hit a parked car and was so glad to stop I didn't feel the pain. Then I did, and called for Mom again. She never came. I walked home, returned the skates, and took a stinging bath. I never cried for Mom again after that.

"Natalie, this way!" John calls.

Part of me wants to ignore him and keep going my own way. But the other part wins out only because I'm too tired.

Home, that part says. I want to go home.

Well, I am a long way from home. John's house is as close as I am going to get today.

I turn and follow him the rest of the way. I am so numb by the end that I bump into John when he stops in the driveway.

"Hey, slow down, why don't you? You should be cooling down now."

Oh, yeah. The god of running again.

I do a quick set of reaches, then head inside.

"You'll cramp up if you do that," he warns from behind me.

I shut the door on whatever he says next and lean against it. My breathing slows down and I feel the adrenaline drifting out of my blood.

Bad letdown.

chapter
SIX

Alice knocks on my door about an hour later. By then I've had a chance to shower and pull on my one clean pair of clothes.

"Yeah?" It feels strange having someone knock on my door. It is Alice's house, not mine, after all. She probably knows the room a whole lot better than I do.

Alice peers in with her hair in curlers. "Do you like pancakes?" she asks.

"Sure." Who doesn't like pancakes?

"Good. Come out while they're hot."

My mouth watering, I hurry out to find Kate and Liz already at the table. Should I sit next to them or not? At the group home I ate standing up most of the time. That way I didn't have to look across at anyone and feel like we had to have a conversation or something.

Finally I sit at the other end of the table, not too close to them, but not so far away that they'll think they must have bad breath.

On the wall across the table, their latest family

picture stares at me. Kate and Liz look like china dolls: pure white and fragile.

John comes in then, a tie flung over his shoulder and his hair still wet. He stops when he sees the pancakes on the griddle.

"Oh. Pancakes." There's a pained expression on his face.

I feel kind of sorry for Alice. Why doesn't her family appreciate her more? Probably just spoiled.

She puts a steaming stack on the table and I reach for them quick. I've never seen pancakes so light and fluffy. But while I am looking around for the syrup I notice everyone is staring at me. I freeze, wondering what I've done.

"We always say a prayer on the food, Natalie, before we eat," Alice says.

Heat spreads across my face. Any hotter and Alice could have fried the pancakes right there. "Oh" is all I can get out.

"Natalie, maybe you'd like to . . . ," John suggests.

It takes me a minute to figure out what he means. What? Me, pray?

"It wouldn't have to be fancy," Alice puts in.

"No," I say. No way in hell. Or in heaven, either.

"Alice, then," John says.

"Our Father," says Alice. The words sound easy to her, like an old lullaby.

I almost fall asleep, but then at the very end of the prayer, Alice includes me. "Please bless Natalie, the newest member of our family. Amen."

There's no rush for the pancakes, so I get two.

"Homemade," Liz whispers to me.

"Mom-made," says Kate.

"How are they?" Alice asks anxiously.

Kate puts a piece in her mouth carefully, without letting it touch her teeth. She closes her lips and jerks backward a second later. Her whole body shakes and she pulls at her throat.

Her lips go bluish, and her eyes bulge out of her head.

I stare around the room, but no one else looks the least bit concerned.

I look back at Kate and see a faint smirk on her foaming lips.

Oh. The acting thing again.

"Katherine," John says, "that was rude. The rest of us can tell when you're acting, but Natalie can't."

With one big breath of air, Kate's face goes back to its normal color. She licks the foam from her lips and shrugs. "Just having a little fun."

She hates me. She doesn't even know me, and already she hates me.

"Ignore her," says Liz. "Kate still thinks she's the baby of the family."

Kate stands up. "Nice try, Mom," she says to Alice,

and takes her plate to the sink with only one bite out of the pancake.

"So what's wrong with them this time? Too much baking soda?" Alice asks.

"That would be my guess," says Kate.

Alice sighs. "My mother always made such perfect pancakes. I don't know why I can't."

"Maybe breakfast just isn't your thing, Mom," says Liz. She doesn't even taste her pancake.

I look down at my plate. The pancakes really do not look bad. And even if they are, this is a golden opportunity to show up Kate. She deserves it.

So I take a bite, and my tongue starts to zing. Whoa. It's like taking a sip of root beer and getting real beer instead. But I keep chewing, keep smiling, keep acting like this is the best thing ever.

I eat the pancakes, even the little crumbs. By the time I'm finished, everyone is staring at me.

"Mmm. Those are really good," I say. "Thanks, Alice. You're a good cook."

"You—you really think so?" says Alice.

I nod vigorously, embarrassed at the look of gratitude on her face.

"She's just not used to having anything but dog food," says Kate.

"I have eaten dog food before." Everyone's eyes freeze on me. "Out of a dog's bowl, too."

There is a long silence.

"That's terrible," says Alice.

Liz makes a soft sound deep in her throat.

"Katherine, go to your room," John says. "I don't want to see you again until you've apologized to Natalie for that remark."

Kate doesn't look too happy. "Fine," she says. "I don't want to go to school today anyway."

Alice puts a hand on John's arm as Kate stomps away. "Are you sure you should have done that?" she asks. "I've been having trouble getting her to school all week as it is."

"Well, maybe you wouldn't have so much trouble with her if you cut her off a little more quickly," says John.

Alice takes a deep breath.

"I don't think that's fair," she says.

John purses his lips. "All right, I'll deal with her," he says. Then he turns to me. "I'm sorry about this, Natalie," he says.

John stands up and goes down the hallway after Kate. Alice picks up the remains of breakfast and clatters the plates in the sink.

"I'll take you to school with Kate and Liz and get you registered," she says.

"Uh—already?" I'd hoped for a bit of a break. School is not my thing. Was one extra day off too much to ask?

33

"We think it would be best to get you going on it right away, so you'll miss as little as possible. You're starting a few weeks late here, but I'm sure you'll be able to catch up."

I'm not so sure.

John comes in later. Kate trails behind him. "Go on," he says.

She comes up to me, right into my face. "Sorry," she mutters.

I don't breathe until she steps away.

"Thank you," says John. "Now, are you ready for school?"

"Almost," says Kate. "I still need a book for English. I have to get it passed off in advance to do a book report on it."

"What, can't you even pick a book for yourself?" asks Liz as she pushes past me and then Kate.

"Ha!" says Kate. And she starts to laugh hysterically, until John gives her a warning look.

"Can you find her a book, please?" he asks Alice. "I've got to get to work."

"Sure."

The front door closes and suddenly I'm alone. Liz is in her room. John has gone to work. Kate and Alice are looking for a book for English. And I am in the kitchen by myself.

I should like it, shouldn't I?

So why do I feel like I have a paper cut doused in lemon juice straight across my chest? It is partly the surprise, I think. You don't expect paper to cut you, you know? It doesn't seem that sharp.

But the blood is there just the same.

chapter
seven

I go back to my room and make sure my duffel is empty so I can load it up with schoolbooks. They always give you a stack of books the first day.

I didn't have a bag at all until the first year of junior high. I found the duffel in the garbage the first week of school. I couldn't see anything wrong with it, so I figured finders keepers, and I brought it home. I wrote my name on it in permanent ink, and the duffel has been mine ever since.

I sit on the bed. Is there anything else I should do? I have a few minutes before school starts.

Curl my hair? Too short by far.

Put on makeup? Having seen Mom put on too much makes me nervous to try. I don't want to end up looking like a raccoon with big lips.

Someone knocks on the door.

"Come in."

Alice. "This is for you."

She hands me a backpack. The nice kind, made of brown leather, with padded straps.

My chest gets tight.

"Well, we should be heading out pretty soon."

"Okay." My fingers play with the little locking clasp on the top part of the pack, closing and opening, closing and opening.

"See you in the car." Alice heads out the door.

"Hey, wait."

"Yes, Natalie?"

"Uh—" This is hard to get out. "Thank you," I say finally.

"For the backpack?" You'd think she's never heard the words before. Well, with Liz and Kate around, maybe she hasn't.

"Yeah," I say. My lips feel like they've been stung by bees, so big and thick I can hardly talk through them.

"You're welcome," Alice says simply. Then she turns and starts down the hallway.

It's stupid to get all sniffy about a backpack.

I'll keep it for now. When I leave the Parkers and go on to wherever I'm going to go, I'll make sure the backpack stays here. That way they can give it to the next girl. It will be real nice for her.

My hands won't let go of it. The leather feels like butter, only it doesn't melt away. It stays there, in my hands.

My backpack.

The sound of Kate and Liz yelling at each other is like a school bell ringing.

Time to go.

I hear Kate and Liz close the front door behind them then.

I walk through the empty house alone. It's like walking through a graveyard. The house is dead without the Parkers.

Does our old apartment feel dead without me and Mom in it? Probably not. It was never alive.

I sit in the front seat of the car with Alice because Liz and Kate are already in back. Besides, I wouldn't have wanted to get squished between them like I was on the couch yesterday.

"You look tense," Alice says as she turns on the ignition.

I shrug. My shoulders are tight and sore. I didn't do enough warming down with my arms, I think. If I tell John, he'll probably tell me it is my own fault.

It is, too.

"Worried about the first day of school?"

"I guess." I think of teachers, the hallways filled with other students, getting dressed for P.E., eating alone in a loud lunchroom. I'd been to two or three schools a year my whole life, which makes about twenty schools in all—if my math is right, which I wouldn't bet on.

You'd think I'd have gotten good at the first day of school thing after all that, but instead it seems to get worse every time. I remember all the other times, and then I can't forget them.

Standing in the wrong line in the lunchroom. Forgetting a towel at gym and having to wipe off with my clothes. Getting my hair caught in the parakeet cage when it used to be long. Being called "Bratalie" at recess. Walking into the boys' bathroom by mistake.

"It's going to be all right," Alice says. "I promise."

I grunt. Yeah, right. She can't promise that. She isn't going to school.

But Alice doesn't give up easily. "You know, Natalie, I remember when I was about your age and I was terrified to start high school. My brothers had told me all these stories about how much homework you get and how—"

"Not that story again," Kate pipes up from the back.

"What's wrong with that story?" asks Alice.

Kate makes a gagging sound.

I think that's the end of the story, but a few blocks down the road, Alice starts up again.

"Well, my brothers were terrible. They filled my locker with sand the first day. I don't know how they got the combination, but they did. The door was stuck and I had to pound and pound to open it. Then all this sand fell out." Alice laughs. "Well, I didn't think it was funny then, let me tell you."

I don't think it sounds funny now, either. It sounds mean. "I thought you said you were adopted."

"I was. My brothers, too. Mom adopted ten of us."

"She adopted ten kids?" Whoa. She was either a crazy person or a saint.

Alice nods. "People just kept asking her if she would take more and she couldn't say no."

My mom used to say kids were too much trouble. She'd never have another kid.

We had a cat once, but it got killed in a fight with another cat. I found it outside our apartment building. The door was all clawed up from the cat trying to get in. Mom and I had both forgotten to wait up for it.

I carried it inside like a baby.

"What are you doing?" asked Mom.

I couldn't answer because I didn't know.

"Take it to the Dumpster." Mom put her hand to her mouth and nose. "It smells so bad it's going to make me puke."

I took the cat out by the bushes and buried it as well as I could without a shovel.

"Just as well it's gone," said Mom when I came back. "Too much trouble."

"Anyway," Alice goes on, "I spent most of that first morning cleaning up the mess my brothers had made."

"Weren't you mad?" I ask.

"I was furious." Alice smiles as she turns onto Main Street. "Actually, the interesting thing was that the rest of my day went a lot easier than I'd expected. I was so mad I forgot all about being afraid. And the day after that, I did my brothers one better."

"You filled their lockers with sand?" I ask.

"Not their lockers," says Alice.

"Their car," say Kate and Liz together, in the back-seat.

It doesn't sound like I'm missing out on much, not having any brothers or sisters. The arguments, the hissy fits, the jealousy, and the practical jokes—big deal, right?

"So, was that the end of it?" I ask.

"Oh, no, no. It went on for years. Every few months there'd be an outbreak and I'd have to retaliate. That's the way it is with brothers. At least, that's the way it was with mine."

"And you still talk to them? I mean, now that you don't have to anymore?"

There's the glint of a tear in Alice's eyes. "They're my brothers," she says.

"And they still play tricks on her," Liz says. "Like they're all teenagers in high school again."

Alice grins. "Wouldn't have it any other way." She wipes at her face, then turns in to the high school parking lot. Liz hops out first, swinging a pink thing over her shoulder that wouldn't hold a pack of gum, let alone any schoolbooks or homework.

"Thanks for the ride, Mom." She blows a kiss at

Alice, then waves at me. "Hope you have a good day, Natalie."

"Thanks," I say, my hands clutching the leather of my backpack so tight it feels like wood instead of butter.

"See you," says Kate, and slams the door without a glance back.

"Sorry about Kate," Alice apologizes. "I could try to get her to apologize but that gets a bit tiresome after a while. It's really her father and me she's mad at, not you. But that's a long story."

"Yeah, well. It doesn't matter." I am not going to be around all that long.

"It does matter," says Alice. "You matter."

I sigh. I don't understand this at all. It's one thing to be in a group home. It's another to have a foster family. The group home was easier.

Alice opens the car door. "I'll show you around a bit. Let's get you registered at the office first." She leads me to a set of double doors at the front of the school.

My hands are cold.

"You look like you're preparing to fight a battle," says Alice as she opens the door.

I try to meet her smile, but it feels like the dentist is prying my mouth open and I need to spit.

chapter
eight

The noise of the school hits me first. The wave of voices pushes me back. The pounding of feet on the floor travels all the way up my spine. My stomach clenches, and I just stop myself from throwing up. This time.

"This way," Alice directs me. I follow, head down.

Inside the office, it's quieter, but every time the door opens, the noise from outside clatters in again.

"Yes?" the secretary asks.

"My foster daughter Natalie needs to register for classes," Alice explains. "It's her first day."

The secretary stares at me through big glasses, like I'm a fly on her fly swatter, red guts spread on green plastic. Ugh.

"You'll need to go see the counselor," she says, pointing to a door on her right.

Inside that office, the counselor tells me I can choose two "electives," but the rest of the classes are assigned. He hands me a list of choices: Spanish, German, French, chorus, band, art, home ec, shop.

"Do I have to take any?" I ask. "I mean, if they're electives?" The thought of getting out of two classes a day makes me excited. Missing out on any school would be good.

"I'm afraid you do," says the counselor. He stares at me, drumming his fingers on the desk.

I can't decide. I scan down the list over and over again, but I just can't make myself say any of the words.

The counselor rubs his bald head. "Mrs. Parker?" he asks finally.

Alice looks at me.

"Please," I say. If John were here, he would love to tell me what to take.

"Well," she says, "Spanish is always useful. And it can't hurt to learn a little cooking. Goodness knows we should have someone in the house who can tell the difference between baking soda and baking powder."

So the counselor types "Spanish" and "home ec" into the computer, and prints out a schedule for me. "You'll need to go to each teacher and make sure they are willing to fit you in," he says. "Also, you should ask what you can do to make up the assignments from the three weeks you've missed so far."

I'm shaking like a leaf. I feel green as a leaf, too. I should have known better than to eat breakfast.

"You want me to stay and help you find each of your classes?" Alice asks.

"No," I say automatically. I don't want her to watch

me make a mess of everything. That would only make it worse.

"I'll come pick you up after school then. At the same place, all right?"

I nod and walk out to the hallway with her.

Tick, tock, tick, tock. Her hips sway to the door.

Then I'm alone. Up to me now. Like it always has been.

I look down at the room number on my first-period class. English. Sorensen. Room 147. I wander for fifteen minutes before I find it.

My arms feel like Jell-O. I can't make one reach up to knock on the classroom door, let alone turn the knob and open it.

The last time I went to an English class was when I was living with Mom and I hadn't read the assigned book. I scribbled out an essay as fast as I could, trying to make something up as I went along. The next day the teacher read the whole thing in front of the class as an example of "the worst piece of writing in the English language" he'd ever seen.

When he gave it back to me, the F on it was as big as the whole paper.

"Hey!"

I turn around and see a girl with short brown hair and a heart-shaped face. She also has long, lean legs that remind me for some reason of John's. I tighten up when she comes close to me.

"The office says there is a new girl in our class. Is that you?"

"I guess so."

"I'm Mary." She puts out her hand.

"Uh. Natalie."

"Come on in. I'll introduce you." She has a sheaf of papers under her arm. "Mrs. Sorensen just sent me out to the office to get some copies. That's how I heard about you."

She is so nice, it is hard not to like her right off, even though I don't want to.

She opens the door and holds it for me. Then she walks me up to the front of the class.

Whoa. There are a lot of faces looking out at me. The front is not my favorite part of the room.

"This is Natalie—" Mary waits for me to add my last name.

"Wills," I say quietly.

"She's new." Like everyone hadn't figured that out already.

"Oh? Did your family just move in?" asks Mrs. Sorensen.

"I'm staying with the Parkers," I try out.

Mrs. Sorensen nods. "Oh. Well, why don't you find a seat?"

Mary points to the third row. "There's one right behind mine."

I walk with her to her desk, then keep walking. I get as far away from Mary's desk as I can.

I tune out most of the lesson. I open the book and turn pages, but I stare at the ceiling and hope Mrs. Sorensen takes the hint.

Either she does or she doesn't notice me in the back. In any case, she doesn't bother me.

The bell rings at the end of class and I make my way to the door. How long will it take me to find my next class? Maybe I should just wait until the halls are cleared and I can breathe easy.

The girl Mary stops me when I step out the door. "I could help you find your next class, if you want," she offers.

She is like John. She doesn't know how to take a hint at all. And she thinks she knows everything about everyone else.

"I don't need your help."

Her face doesn't crumple. She doesn't even wince. Mary just stares at me like she can see straight through my skin to the clicking brain beyond. Then she nods, and goes on her way.

I'm thirty minutes late to the next class, Spanish, and I don't understand a word of what they are saying. But I try to concentrate anyway, because if I don't, the look on Mary's face will come back to me.

What worries me most about her is that I know

she won't give up. She's too thick-skinned. Thin-skinned people are a lot easier to get rid of. Thick-skinned people keep coming back for more, like a dog who remembers the last time you gave him food.

A memory hits me. Mom, standing at the door, listening to a salesman. I don't remember what he was selling, but when he tried to hand a brochure to Mom, she wouldn't take it. It dropped to the floor and he picked it back up, going right on with his speech, his eyes turning to me.

"Now all you have to do is give me your name and I'll sign you up."

Mom stared at him.

"Mrs. . . ." He started writing.

Mom grabbed his notebook and yanked off the first page.

"Hey!"

Mom pulled off another page.

"I need those, lady."

A third page and the guy understood. He went away quietly and he didn't come back.

Mom might not be the yelling type, but she lets you know if she doesn't want you around.

chapter
nine

After school, Alice picks me up right on time.

"Kate is staying after school this week for drama, Liz for debate. I'll come back and get them later," she says.

I sit in the backseat and lean my head against the window. It has been raining since this morning, and the sun is just starting to come out. The droplets on the glass are like miniature colored jewels.

One bright blue one reminds me of the ring Mom's last boyfriend gave her. He was a dealer, which meant he could give Mom a discount on her stuff. Maybe that's all she saw in him.

She thought the ring was great that night, went on and on about it.

"Isn't it incredible?" She shoved it in my face so close I could hardly see it.

"Sure," I said. "Great."

"Can you believe he gave it to me? He must really love me."

"Yeah, Mom. I'm sure he does."

DuBOIS

"Maybe we'll get married. Would you like that, Nat? You'd have a new dad and a new dress."

Like they were about the same.

"You'd love that, wouldn't you?"

"Love it, Mom."

Finally, she went to sleep.

In the morning, she woke up and got herself some coffee. After her first cup, she stared at the cheap gold-painted ring, and started to cry. It took her a few tries to get it off her finger. Then she ran into the kitchen and turned on the disposal. Chunk-chunk, and it was gone.

"Natalie?" Someone's shaking my shoulder.

"Huh?" I sit bolt upright, knocking my nose on the cold window in the process.

"You fell asleep on the way home." Alice's face comes in and out of focus. "You'll freeze if you stay out here, though. You can go back to sleep inside, if you want. At least until the social worker comes."

The image of Ms. Beck drives all hope of sleep away. I teeter inside. I'm starving.

"There are crackers in the cupboard," Alice says, coming in behind me.

Can she read minds?

"Or I can make you up an egg, if you'd rather."

"Uh—" I think about breakfast.

"I can make a decent fried egg, you know."

I still hesitate.

"Canned soup?" Alice tries. "But I'll have to do it quick because Ms. Beck said she'd be here around four o'clock."

"All right," I say. Thirty minutes and Ms. Beck will be here. Staring at me. Asking me questions. Trying to figure me out.

Alice cuts me a piece of fresh homemade bread to go with the soup. It falls into pieces in her hands as she tries to butter it. "I can't figure out why this doesn't stick together," she mutters.

I try to think back on what we learned in home ec today. We're actually doing a section right now on breads and muffins, but I can't think of anything the teacher said.

Blah, blah, blah went her mouth.

Buzz, buzz, buzz went my brain.

After eating the whole pan of soup, I go into my room to wait for Ms. Beck. I should be looking through all my late homework assignments, but instead I sit on my bed and stare at the ceiling. Lisa and I used to do that together sometimes. Then Sharon would come in and start tickling us. Once she tried a naughty joke. "There were three men in an elevator when the power went off."

I put my hands over my ears.

Sharon came over and pulled them off. "Listen to this one. It's funny."

"I don't want to."

"What's wrong with a little laughing?" asked Sharon. "Don't we deserve a little laughing, in here?"

I didn't say anything for a long time. Then I let it out. "Feels too much like crying," I said. "Like I'm losing control." Sharon didn't laugh as much after that.

The doorbell rings and I hear Ms. Beck's shrill voice coming closer. Does she have to come in my room? I meet her at the door, hoping to steer her toward the living room.

"Thanks, Mrs. Parker," says Ms. Beck. "I'll talk to her in here. I want to give her a chance to say whatever she feels in private."

So Alice goes away and I have to let Ms. Beck sit down in the chair by my desk while my legs back up against the bed. My feet are aching from walking around at school and my arms are still stiff from not stretching out after the run this morning, but I'm not going to lie down on the bed like I'm visiting a psychiatrist. I may have problems, but I'm not crazy.

"So," says Ms. Beck. "How are you doing?"

"Fine," I say.

"Are you starting to fit in with your new family?"

Fit in? She makes me sound like a building block. Just find the right hole and drop me in.

But Ms. Beck doesn't notice I haven't answered her. She goes right on with her questions. She probably has a list of them she has to get through.

"Do you like your foster sisters?"

"They're fine," I say.

"How about Mr. and Mrs. Parker?"

"Fine," I say again.

"And your room? Your new school?"

"Fine, fine."

Ms. Beck puts down her notebook and looks at me closely. "You know, you're a very lucky girl."

Me, lucky? "What do you mean?"

"Not every foster family is like the Parkers."

"I know," I say. I really don't want her to go on about all the terrible foster families in the world. I've heard plenty at the home.

"I went running with John this morning," I volunteer, to distract her.

She zooms in on that. "Oh? And how did you like that?"

I shrug.

"Do you think you'll keep doing that?" She looks hopeful.

"No."

"Why not?"

I stare at her.

"I like to run alone."

"What about your mother?"

My face gets cold and nerveless.

"Do you think about her a lot?"

"No," I say. I stare her right in the eye.

"You don't think about her at all?"

"I didn't say that."

"You think about her some of the time, then."

I shrug again.

She makes a sound like a horse. "Natalie, you're not making this easy for me."

Yeah, that was the whole point.

"So, if you think about her some of the time, Natalie, what do you think?"

There's no way I'm going to tell her about the dream. But I have to tell her something.

"She's messed up," I admit.

"And what exactly do you mean by that?" asks Ms. Beck.

What, she wants a definition or something? "I mean she can't take care of me right now."

Did she ever take care of me?

I think suddenly of a song she used to sing me, when she put me to sleep. I can feel her hand on my cheek, rubbing it. And the music—Mom's no great singer—but I always felt safe when she sang that song. No matter how many bad things had happened during the day, if Mom sat with me at night and sang, I didn't care. That was all I wanted from her.

I wish I could open my window and get some air.

"Do you believe she will be able to take care of you again?"

A dribble of sweat runs down my face, onto my lips, to my chin. It holds there for just a second, before dropping to my shirt.

"Natalie?" asks Ms. Beck. "Did you hear what I said?"

If I say I think Mom won't ever be able to take care of me, then Ms. Beck will write that down. Maybe some judge will read it and then tell Mom what I said. It would kill her.

If I tell her I do think she'll be able to take care of me, then she'll write that down, too. And then I'll get sent back to her.

Not that I don't want to go. I do, but . . .

"I don't know," I say, as breathless as I had been at the top of the hill that morning.

"Well, that's honest, at least. Maybe the first honest answer you've given me today." Ms. Beck smiles. She looks younger when she smiles. Also, a few hairs have come out of her bun and are frizzing up around her eyes. That makes her look more human.

Maybe that's why I decide to ask her a real question. "Can you always tell if people are lying to you?"

She blinks wide blue eyes at me. "Well, that's part of my job. I'm no mind reader. But I do my best. And people give clues. The way they move. Not just their words. I've been figuring it out as I go along. It's not exactly something they teach at school."

It's a relief to hear she doesn't think school's useful, either. Maybe she's not so bad, after all.

"I've been wrong, too," she admits. "Some people are just so used to lying. I think maybe they don't know what's truth and what isn't anymore. And other people know the truth and are trying desperately to live up to it."

Is she talking about my mom? I don't dare ask.

She tells me anyway. "Your mom, for example. She's working hard to stay clean and she's working through some issues in therapy. She really misses you."

There's this football in my throat and I can't get it down. I swallow and swallow, but it doesn't move.

"What do you think about that?"

I am shaking all over, so cold even though there's sweat pouring onto my chin now. You'd think I was running a marathon.

"She'd like to have some contact with you."

"What does that mean?" I try to keep my voice even and low, but it squeaks on the last word.

"Well, you wouldn't necessarily have to meet her, if that's what you're afraid of. You could talk to her on the phone or write her a letter, even. Whatever you feel up to."

"Uhhh—"

"You don't have to decide right now, either. But she asked me to ask you."

"She did?"

Ms. Beck pats down the front of her tailored black jacket, then waves good-bye to me. "We'll talk next month, all right?"

I can't even move enough to nod at her, or to stand and walk her to the door.

All I can think of is that she might have had something from my mom in her pocket that very minute.

I have this urge to run after her and yell at her to give it to me, but I stop myself. I can't decide if I'd rip it up into tiny pieces and feed it to the fire or put it in a nice beveled wood frame right above my bed so I can read it every night and remember that I had a mother once. I might have one again.

chapter
ten

Alice orders out for pizza that night.

"Heavy food to run on," John says, with a meaningful look at me.

I eat five pieces just to spite him, and go to bed with my stomach stretched to its limit, my head pounding.

In the morning John's alarm goes off and he starts his warm-up in the foyer. I'm not asleep and I'm not going back to sleep. I think about the pump of fresh air in my lungs and the challenge of climbing a hill, but I don't get out of bed. Not even when I hear John walk through the hallway and stop in front of my door. Finally he's gone.

I open my window and stick my head out into the clear cold. I do a couple stretches on the floor of my room to get my blood moving, then head into the shower. The heat warms me like a good run, but I don't get the adrenaline rush I did yesterday. Just as well, I tell myself. You don't want to get addicted to it.

After a breakfast of burned toast, Alice offers to drive me and Kate and Liz to school.

"No thanks, Mom," says Kate. "The bus gets me there on time."

"I've got a ride," says Liz.

Alice looks at me, eyebrows raised.

"Uh—I guess I'll try the bus." I have to get used to it sometime, don't I?

Kate walks up to the bus stop with me, and we stand on the dewy grass together. She doesn't say anything rude. She doesn't say anything nice, either, but I'll count this as progress. Maybe she's figured out I'm not going to mess anything up for her. It's her family, not mine.

As soon as she gets on the bus, though, she finds a group of friends to sit by and leaves me. I watch her go, then sit in the front. Her voice in the back of the bus is like the bass of a big boom box.

"Yeah, she thinks she's from the big city. You know, looks down on us about everything. Like she's the queen of fashion."

There's a wall of laughter coming at me. It hits, makes my face go red. I try not to listen anymore, but I've heard enough to stare down at my clothes and see how old they are. They never were that nice and now they're worse.

At the next stop, a girl sits down next to me. She keeps staring at my short hair like someone came and buzzed a crop circle in it during the night.

Finally we get to school. The halls are twice as crowded as the bus and there's no way to get "off."

At noon, I don't want to go to the lunchroom or wait in line, so I buy an apple from the "à la carte" and chomp it down on the way to my next class. By the end of the day I'm so tired of sitting, standing, and moving next to other people that I don't even go near the buses. I'm determined to walk home myself.

I realize after about an hour that I am lost. In Salt Lake City I could never get lost, because the mountains were always there to the east.

Here in Heber, there are mountains everywhere, north, south, east, and west. Maybe someone who'd lived here forever would be able to tell the difference between the ones behind John and Alice's house and the others, but I can't.

I could stop at one of the little farmhouses along the road and ask for help, but I'm not that eager to get home. The air is cool as a piece of double-mint gum, and except for the occasional anonymous rumbling of a semitruck, it's quiet. So I keep going, down this road, turn here, then there. Wherever it seems most deserted, I go.

I reach the skirt of one of the mountain ranges. It's beautiful here. Everyone thinks of fall colors as red and yellow and orange, but there are a lot more than that. Some trees have turned bright purple, some are still a deep, dark green, and there are blue spruces poking their heads out all around. If you tried to paint it I bet people would say it looked unreal.

I get off the dirt road and find a cubbyhole behind a big bush. I sit very still and watch the clouds morph from cotton to kangaroos across the sky. A family of rabbits crosses the trail ahead of me, a big one first, then the smaller ones. Dad and the kids out for a walk.

I think about staying up here and not going back, but then John will come after me. And somehow, he'll find me.

When it starts to get cool, I head away from the mountain realizing I'll have to find a phone to call Alice. But before I reach the first house on the asphalt, I see a group of teenage runners heading up the hill. Behind them all is this old guy without any hair and a bit of a gut. Why is he running with them?

I step off to the side to let them pass me. They don't jog. They run, like John. I turn to watch them zip up the hill I've just come down.

Suddenly I am almost clipped by someone coming up from behind. I have the vague impression of dark hair and long legs.

It's Mary, the girl from my English class. She looks more like she's dancing than running.

How far is it from here to the school? Maybe four or five miles out, if you go straight instead of in all the nooks and crannies like I did walking. And they're not finished. By the time they head back, they'll have run twelve miles or more.

Half a marathon.

"You're slowing down, Coach," Mary teases, her voice carrying clear in the canyon.

"Don't worry about me, Mary," the coach calls back. He puts on enough speed to catch up to her for a while.

Mary disappears behind a switchback, then reappears. Her hair keeps hanging into her face. I wonder how she can stand it, but I don't see her ever push it back.

Finally I can't see her anymore. Or the coach or any of the rest of the team.

They should be a movie. One of those constantly playing things, so you can see it over and over again. I'd never get tired of it.

Pure happiness. Pure motion.

That's what I try to get at when I run.

I stumble away, feeling empty inside. Mary and the others and the coach—they all have something that I don't have, something that I will never have. I was built without it.

"You're a natural." John's words stutter over and over again in my head. *"You ever think of joining a team?"*

He's wrong. I'm not a natural. I'm a monster.

I make myself knock on the door of a two-story log cabin–style house with the lights on and ask if I can use the phone. I live through a few questions and a sympathetic look from the woman of the house.

Maybe she can see the hole inside me, too. But I can't ask her what it is or how to fill it.

I call Alice and tell her where I am.

"Oh, Natalie. I was so worried about you." Her voice wavers, like Mom's when she's out of money. "What happened?"

I don't even have words to explain it. "I got lost," I say. "That's all."

"Why didn't you take the bus? Or call me?"

I didn't want to.

"I didn't think," I say.

"Where are you? I'll come get you right now." I can hear Kate and Liz shouting at each other in the background, and it sounds like Alice is standing over the stove, burning something in a big pan.

I tell her the address the woman who opened the door wrote down for me.

"You're in Charleston?" asks Alice.

"Yeah. So?"

"You walked all that way? By yourself?"

What—she thinks I flew? "Yeah."

"That's past Midway. Natalie, you're two towns away."

"Oh." I try not to feel stupid. "It didn't seem that far coming out. If I knew where I was, I could probably still walk home."

"No!" says Alice. "Natalie, you stay right there. Do you hear me?"

"I hear you," I say. Then I hang up the phone and stand there, fidgeting, until the doorbell rings. I forget this isn't my house and run for it. Alice is already saying thanks to the woman, and I duck around the two of them and hop into the back of the car.

"I'll come pick you up tomorrow," Alice offers as we drive away.

I shake my head. "I'll ride the bus."

"It's not that much of a hassle, really, Natalie."

She's making me feel smaller and smaller. "I don't need you to," I say.

The rest of the drive home is quiet. I check the odometer and realize it's a ten-mile drive.

"Natalie," says Alice, when we're coming into the driveway.

"What?"

"It's okay." Her voice is sleepy-soft.

"What's okay?" I ask.

"Needing something. Or someone."

Her saying that makes me feel sick to my stomach and so dizzy I can hardly keep myself upright in the car. I hold tight to the door handle and focus.

"You don't have to do everything yourself," Alice says.

"I always have before," I say. And what if I have to again?

"I know," says Alice. "But you have us now. Me and John and Liz and—well, we're working on Kate."

I tense up at that. "She doesn't have to—" I start to say.

"Yes, she does," says Alice. "Because you're part of the family now."

Yeah, I think, but for how long?

Alice reaches for the door.

I go inside a step or two behind Alice, my muscles aching all over. No warm-up or -down before my long walk today. I'll pay for that later, and I'll probably have to listen to a lecture from John about it.

In the kitchen, Alice motions me toward a plate of cookies on the counter.

They're chocolate chip, my favorite. I reach for one, then remember Alice can't cook.

"One of my church friends baked these for me," Alice explains. She takes a bite in demonstration. "They're really good."

I take one. It's still soft and greasy on the bottom. "Delicious," I say after one bite. The cookie's gone in two, and I'm reaching for another one a moment after that.

Alice stops me at three. "You don't want to ruin your dinner."

Kate comes in before I can argue that I won't, that I'm a bottomless pit today, after all that walking.

"Those Sister Kelly's?" she asks, pointing to the cookies.

"Yes," says Alice, swatting her away. "You can have one after we eat."

Kate makes her voice high and nasal. "You let her have some," she complains.

"She needed one," says Alice. "And you don't."

Kate mutters something that I don't catch, but her look at me is pretty clear. Alice asks her to set the table, and then Liz comes in with a report on her latest debate tournament. She's arguing about the role of government in the disintegration of the family.

John comes in just as Liz is done and gives Alice a kiss. "What's for dinner?" he asks.

"Spaghetti," she says.

"Ahhh, spaghetti," says John. "I love spaghetti."

Alice elbows him in the stomach. "That's because it's the only thing I know how to cook."

I wait for Kate to gag or Liz to laugh, but neither of them does.

I guess I don't know them that well, after all.

chapter
eleven

I'm in the laboratory again, but this time I'm not strapped to the table. Instead, I'm on a treadmill, running and running but never going anywhere. The air rushes straight through me, chilling me to the bone. My legs are roped together with just enough space for me to keep going at a decent pace. There's none of the free feeling I have when I go running.

Then I look down and see the skin of my chest is split open like a cadaver's in an anatomy class. I can see my heart pumping along just fine, my lungs expanding and contracting with each breath. I can even see my stomach kneading up food as it gurgles happy sounds. But there's no blood, anywhere. I'm all drained out.

No wonder I think something is missing. It is. Maybe someone will come to fix me.

Then John walks in wearing a lab coat that used to be on my mom. He has two pairs of glasses, one across his nose and one on top of his head. He has eyes in both places, too.

"My monster," he says. "My running monster."

No, I want to tell him. I'm not your monster. But I'm running too hard to talk.

John checks the controls on the treadmill. He adjusts one knob, and suddenly the treadmill is going twice as fast as before. I am losing ground with every step. It won't be long until I'm thrown off. I look for a way to cut the ropes around my feet. There's a wall of knives on my right, butcher knives, pocket knives, paring knives—every kind of knife you can think of. I reach over, grab a cleaver from the wall, and fling it at John.

It catches him right in the middle of the chest, opening him just the way I am. Then he starts to bleed, which ruins the view of his fluttering heart and lungs. He tries to push the blood back inside, but it just gets all over his fingers and drips onto the floor. He collapses into the spreading puddle.

"Why, Natalie?" he calls to me. "Why? You know I did the very best I could."

I wake up with my heart racing. The quilt on my bed is wrapped around my legs. I put my hands to my nightshirt and feel around for holes. Then, just to be sure, I peek underneath and sigh at the sight of my whale-belly-white skin.

It takes me a long time to get back to sleep. I think about what John said to me in the dream: *"I did the very best I could."* It is his deep, uneven voice, but the words are Mom's. She said them the night before child protective services came to take me away. I think she must have known they would come the next morning. The lights were off because she hadn't paid the utility bill and she hadn't been to either work or therapy for weeks. So she didn't go out that night. She didn't get herself her usual beer out of the fridge. Instead, she sat on the couch next to me, massaging my shoulders so hard I had to bite my lip not to tell her to stop.

"I don't know if I've been a good mother to you or not, Natalie," she said, and slid over next to me so I could lean my head on her shoulder.

She was a good mother right then. She didn't have to run with me or make me pancakes for breakfast or drive me to school or do any of the things that John and Alice did for Kate and Liz.

"But I want you to know that I did the very best I could," Mom said. She planted a kiss right on my nose, warm and soft. If only she stayed with me like that, touched me, made sure I knew that she was there. I would have been happy with that.

I think it was easier for her when I was little. Like the day she took me to Liberty Park. I rolled in the grass down a hill, then ran all the way up so that she could catch me at the bottom all over again. She hugged me over and over again that day: after she locked our apartment door, on the way to the park, twice at the park, and then again on the way back. She hugged me at home, too, after she handed me an ice-cream cone for a treat—vanilla, our favorite. And when I dropped it and started to cry, she hugged me again, for a long time.

There are so many bad memories of her, I had forgotten that there were good ones, too. I wish I hadn't remembered them now, either. My chest feels like it's open again, my heart spilling out from between my ribs. I breathe in short bursts, holding back the tears. Tears can't help fix things, any more than the dream-doctor John can.

Only Mom can.

And Mom said she'd already done the best she could.

chapter twelve

It's Friday and I get to English early. It's a mistake.

Mary spots me as she walks in the door.

"Natalie, right?" She comes up and leans over my desk.

I nod.

"I thought I saw you last night, over in Charleston. I should have stopped and said hi, but I was too busy trying to keep up."

Since she takes every other opportunity to bother me, I am glad she was busy last night.

"So, did you run all the way out there?" she asks.

"I walked," I say.

"Same thing," she says, with this gleam in her eyes like she's just found her long-lost identical twin sister.

I lift my hands and my voice is sharp. "It isn't. I'm not that good of a runner. Really."

She just smiles. "You could be. You just need practice. Why don't you come run with us? I'll bet you'd have a great time. We meet right after school at the track."

"No," I say flatly.

"Oh." Her smile fades. "I just thought—"

"Look, I said no and I mean no."

She sighs. "Well, if you change your mind . . ."

The bell rings and everyone gets quiet for a while. There's no sign of Mrs. Sorensen, though. Just when we're all looking around, trying to decide if we're going to stay, the principal walks in.

"I'm sorry, but Mrs. Sorensen has been hospitalized for a broken leg and won't be back to school for another week. Mr. Landers is going to substitute starting on Monday. For today, Mrs. Sorensen said you were to turn in your work from chapter three and start on the questions for chapter four. Any questions?"

He stares around the room.

After he walks out there's a moment of silence, then people start chatting in a dull roar.

"Landers?" The boy just in front of me says. I think his name is Thomas. "The bald guy with the gut?"

Mary turns around, her neck tight except for the vein pumping blue on the side. "He's in good shape," she says.

"Yeah, right. That's why he hangs over his pants like that," Thomas returns. "I'll bet he's doing a really great job coaching the cross-country team." He puffs out his cheeks and wipes at his face, then sinks into his desk chair. "Oh, I'm so tired. You go on ahead."

A bunch of people laugh. Not me, though. I saw Coach Landers running for myself.

Mary stands up and walks to the boy's seat.

"I'd like to see you in a race against him. When do you think you'd be ready? Next millennium?" She pokes Thomas in his soft stomach. The whole class laughs.

"Ha, ha. Very funny. Look, I take it back. He's an Olympic athlete. He's an iron man. He's going to win a triathlon this year."

Not the most sincere apology, but Mary's neck relaxes.

Mary opens up her book and starts reading. By the time the bell rings to let us out, she's gotten halfway through chapter five. I'm still stuck on the first poem in chapter four. Poetry is not my thing.

I wait until the other kids file out; then I go to the bathroom. Mary is just coming out of one of the stalls.

"So, how are you doing, Natalie?"

"Fine," I say. What do I have to do to shake her off?

She moves to the sink and starts washing her hands.

"Just a friendly warning: Stay away from the school lunch today."

She's talking about school lunch?

"It's Mexican surprise casserole."

"Yeah?" I wonder what's surprising about it. Probably the heartburn.

"It'll be like lead in your stomach. Takes a full day before you can run again. Believe me, I know."

"Like you know about Coach Landers?" I say. Why did I do that? I'm encouraging her to talk.

But the truth is, I'm curious about Coach Landers. First John and now Mary both talking about him. What is he, a hero or something?

"Yeah," she says, "I know about Coach Landers."

It's the perfect opportunity for her to overwhelm me with information, and she doesn't.

Fine. I can live with that.

I head for the door.

"He saved my life, you know." She says it so quietly I can hardly hear her.

Go on, I tell myself, leave now. This is my last chance not to get involved with her, and I know it.

"Saved your life how?" I ask. I lean against the wall next to the sink.

Mary stares at herself in the mirror. "Got me running," she says. "Instead of—" She stops talking.

"Drugs?" I ask.

She blushes bright red. "How did you know that?" She stares down at her arms, like she's looking for old tracks.

"My mom was a user," I say.

Mary's head jerks up. "Oh, yeah?"

74

"Is a user." It's not like she's dead. Not yet, anyway.

"That's why you're with the Parkers?" Mary asks.

I nod.

"You think she'll get cleaned up?"

"Maybe."

"Well, I hope so. Not that I want you to go away or anything." She stumbles over the words.

"Thanks," I say.

"You know why she started?"

"No." I only know she couldn't stop.

"Well, I got into it because—well, for lots of reasons," Mary says. "I didn't think anyone cared. But Coach Landers happened to see me out late one night and told me he'd be by my house the next morning to take me running. He said I'd better be ready because I was going whether I wanted to or not."

A strange quiver shoots up my spine, like I've just started the climb up a roller coaster.

"I just blew him off, didn't get home till five A.M. He was right there in his car with the other runners. They were all waiting for me."

"Whoa."

"Coach Landers doesn't let anything stop him," says Mary. "He just goes and does what needs to be done."

The cynic in me rises. "Well, he just wanted you on his team," I say. "You're a great runner."

Mary turns away from the mirror and stares at me.

"I'm a great runner because Landers is a great coach."

Then she walks away.

I don't even think about class until I've already missed Spanish. I just keep thinking about Landers and Mary. What will she do if she ever finds out he's not all he's cracked up to be?

I've felt that way and I don't want to see it happen to her. I don't know if she could take seeing her hero fall.

chapter thirteen

That night, I am sitting in my room after dinner when there's a knock at the door. I get up and open it. John and Alice look very serious.

"Can we come in?" asks John.

"Um—yeah." They're sending me back to the group home. Just when I'm getting used to them, they've decided they can't take me, after all. They don't want a monster for a kid.

I sit on my bed and wonder why I care. I want to go anyway, to get away from Mary and her problems, and from Kate and hers. Don't I?

John takes the chair by my desk and Alice eases down next to me on the bed, close but not quite touching.

"What's—up?" My voice breaks in the middle.

"We're just wondering how school is going for you," John says. "Any problems?"

"No, not really." I press my hands against the bed to steady myself.

"Well, I remember Ms. Beck saying that you hated math. If you need any help, I taught it not too many years ago. Some kids even said they liked it, after I showed them the ins and outs."

"I'm never going to like math," I say. Is that what he came here to talk about? Math?

Maybe they're not sending me back to the group home. A leaf of hope flutters above me and I want to grab at it, but I'm afraid.

John pushes up his glasses and licks his lips nervously.

"Actually, we have something else we want to talk to you about," Alice puts in.

"What?"

"Well," says Alice.

"We noticed that it's your birthday next week," he says. "And we wondered what kind of a celebration you'd like to have."

My muscles go hard all over. "Nothing," I say, my jaw tight. I wish they hadn't brought it up at all. I hate birthdays even more than math.

"Are you sure?" Alice goes on. "I could order a cake from the store so you don't have to risk health hazards with mine. You could even invite some friends from school, if you'd like to have a party."

"I don't want a party," I say to them. I don't have any friends, I say to myself.

"Why not?" John asks. Push, push, push.

"Birthdays are for kids," I say. That's what I've told myself since I turned five and waited all day for someone to say anything that would make me certain I had actually been born.

Last year on my birthday, Mom tried to fly off the balcony. When I caught her she got mad and smacked me hard in my eye. "Mom, it's me. Natalie," I said.

"You're holding me back, dragging me down," she whimpered. But she let me pull her a few steps from the edge.

"It's all right, Mom. It's going to be all right." I stroked her arm, feeling the soft blond hairs move back and forth. Mom breathed softly. I thought it was over and relaxed.

Just then Mom swung at me a second time.

She missed, but only barely. Then she collapsed and I dragged her into bed.

By morning my right eye was swollen shut. Some birthday present. As I looked in the mirror in the cold light of day, I wished she'd gotten both my eyes. Then I wouldn't have had to see how awful I looked.

The birthday before that wasn't much better. Mom came home late from work—she was working then. She didn't say anything about my birthday. There weren't any presents or a birthday cake. She didn't even buy me a lousy card.

Instead she ate some of the macaroni and cheese I'd cooked for dinner. Then she told me how my father sent her flowers on the day I was born.

"They were white roses, my favorite."

I always thought her favorites were lilacs, but I didn't say it.

"I waited and waited for him to come. I told them no drugs. I wanted to talk to him the way I really was."

Wow. Mom saying no to drugs. She must really have been desperate.

"He never did come, though. I think a kid was just too heavy for him. You know?"

"Yeah," I said. Not so light for her, either.

I look back to John and Alice.

"A party would be so nice for you," Alice persists.

I am expecting a fight from John, too, and I'm ready to turn on the freeze.

But John just shakes his head and holds up his hands at Alice. "It's her birthday, Alice. She should have some say in what she wants."

Alice sighs. "You're sure? No party?"

"No party," I say.

Then she and John walk out together.

I lie back on the bed, my fists clenched at my sides. It would have been better if they'd come in to tell me about going back to the group home. At least there we didn't celebrate birthdays. It was Sharon's a week before I left. She got to pick what was for dinner, and we had chocolate ice cream for dessert, but that was it. No singing. No candles. No presents.

No disappointment, either.

chapter
fourteen

Saturday I wait in bed for the sound of John's alarm, debating again about going jogging with him. But the alarm never goes off. I guess John sleeps in on the weekends. I wonder if Mary does, too, or if she and the rest of the track team at school spend extra time running on Saturday. Would they reach the top of the mountain today? Would they look down and see how small we all are?

I drift off until long past breakfast, then stay in my room as much as possible until Kate comes to get me for dinner.

She just opens my door and stares at me.

"What?"

She points to the kitchen, and starts to walk away.

"Oh." What is wrong with her anyway?

"I don't get it," I say loudly.

She turns, a superior look on her face. "What don't you get?"

"You," I say.

Her lips twist. "Hey, I'm an actress. What I do is

purely for effect." She says each word precisely, like she's on stage, speaking to carry her lines across an audience.

But today she only has an audience of one. So why is she trying so hard?

"You already have everything anyone could ever want," I say. "So why do you have to be such a—"

"A what?" she asks.

I swallow the word she really deserves and say, "A jerk," instead.

"You think you have a monopoly on all the pain in the world?" she attacks, eyes blazing. "Well, you don't."

Oh, yeah. She has such pain.

Kate stomps on the floor. I worry she's going to press her heel into my bare foot, and I pull it back.

"Look, I've been living here all my life. I know my family. You don't."

"So?"

"So, Mom and Dad almost got divorced five years ago. And now they act like they're the perfect parents. They expect me and Liz to act like we're the perfect kids, too."

"Well, maybe they got over things eventually," I say.

"Yeah," she sneers. "And maybe I'm not the only actress in the family."

"Or maybe you act so much you can't tell the difference between pretend and real," I say.

"Oh." Kate laughs. "And you can?"

I want to sling something back, but Alice interrupts us.

"Is there a problem here?" she asks. Kate and I have squared off to different corners of the room.

I turn away. "No," I say.

"Kate?"

"No problem." Kate is instant perfect daughter. She smiles at me, and then at Alice. "I was just telling her it was time for dinner." She leaves smoothly on that exit line.

Alice stares at me. "Really no problem?" she asks.

"Really," I say. If Alice had to choose sides between me and her own daughter, there'd be no contest. Kate would win every time.

"Okay, then. Let's go in to dinner."

I walk close behind Alice, and don't have to look at Kate until we get to the table. She's still in character. All smiles. All perfect.

When we're finished eating, Liz gets up. "I've got some research to get through."

"Wait a minute," says Alice. "I think we should spend some time together tonight."

Liz groans.

Kate's smile falls off one side of her mouth, then twitches.

"Quality family time," says Alice, looking at John. "I think we really need that today. Smooth out some wrinkles, you know?"

"All right," he says.

So John goes to the TV room and brings back a couple of board games.

Monopoly. Gag.

Career. Double gag.

Life. Vomit.

Alice points to Life.

John hands everyone a car.

"But maybe Natalie should play on someone's team," says Kate. "I'll bet she's never played any board games before. Have you, Natalie?"

I say, "They have lots of old games at the group home." We had a group night when we had to do something together, and with board games you just had to pass the dice. No conversation. No staring.

"But you didn't have games at home, I'll bet," says Kate.

"Kate," says John with a warning tone.

"Just asking. I want to get to know Natalie better. So tell me, Natalie."

I push the spinner to her. "Go," I say.

Kate turns out very rich, but unhappy.

"Hey, life has winners and life has losers," I say. I walk slowly back to my room.

I don't realize Kate is following me until I reach for the light and she touches my arm.

I jump. "What do you want?" I ask.

"Hey," says Kate. "It's just a game." She smiles her fake smile and runs off.

For her it's a game. But for me, it's not.

chapter
fifteen

Sunday morning Alice peeks in while I'm still in my pajamas.

"I'm sorry this is such late notice. We have church at nine. If you'd like to come, you're welcome."

"Uh. I don't think so," I tell her. She's letting me go easy this time, giving me an actual choice. If only she'd give me a choice about school. I could survive without ever leaving the house.

"All right—if you're sure?"

"I'm sure."

The last time I went to a church was when one of Mom's friends died of an overdose. I remember staring at her in the casket, thinking she was so beautiful. She had gorgeous black hair, long and curly, falling over her pale face.

"Why?" I asked Mom.

"Bad luck," said Mom. "Just bad luck."

It wasn't a good enough answer for me.

After Alice leaves, I hear showers, hair dryers,

clicking high heels. I get up after a car engine fades away in the distance. The table is still scattered with the remains of breakfast. I grab a bowl of cereal and pour on some milk, then dig in.

When I'm finished, I load dishes into the dishwasher. That was one of my jobs at the group home, so I'm pretty good at it.

After that, it's still only 9:15 and Alice said they wouldn't be back until noon.

Three hours of church. Three hours to myself.

So—what to do?

I wander for a while, just to see what I can see.

It's rude, I know, but I can't help myself. I want to know about Alice and John and I want to know things that I can't ask them. What was the trouble about? How long were they separated? How did they get back together?

I rummage through their medicine cabinets first. I don't know what I think I will find. It looks like Alice has her side, with aspirin, Tylenol, Pamprin, cold medication, some Band-Aids, and a thermometer. John's side has an electric razor. That's it. No deep, dark secrets there.

I poke around their closets, too. John's has a bunch of button-down shirts in different colors, an assortment of conservative ties on a little tie rack, and one really wild Hawaiian shirt that I'll bet he never wears.

I try Alice's closet next. It's stuffed so full I can hardly get the door open to look inside. The floor is covered with shoes that might or might not have matches. She has a bunch of skirts and dresses pushed to the side—they probably don't fit her any-more. They look pretty small to me. She has sweaters thrown up on the top shelf, some tacky, some nice.

I push the door open a little more and see a wooden jewelry box peeking out from underneath one sweater. Aha! She wouldn't put it up there unless it was important.

I go into the kitchen to get a stool to reach it. On the way through the hallway that leads to the foyer, I lock the front door—just in case. I know John has keys to open it, but it will give me a little time if someone does come back early.

I freeze right there in the foyer at that thought, my hand on the doorknob. Could this be the test? Maybe they aren't really at church. Maybe they are planning to sneak back into the house and see what I'm doing.

Or they could have set up video cameras in the bedrooms—wherever I'm not supposed to be.

I'm almost eating my heart, it's so high in my throat. I swallow it down, then walk to the back door and lock it, too. Then I search the house, every nook and cranny. No one is there. I know I'm being para-noid, but I can't help it.

It's 11:00 when I go back to Alice and John's room and climb up on the stool to get the jewelry box down.

First drawer. Earrings—clip-ons, because Alice doesn't have pierced ears. A ring with the stone fallen out of it. A fancy hair clip in a butterfly design, the wings dotted with what looks like crushed diamonds.

Second drawer. A pearl necklace with a matching bracelet. They look real. Expensive, too. But what do I know about jewelry? I've never seen any except Mom's fake ring that she threw in the garbage disposal.

I try the pearls on and look in the full-length mir-ror on Alice's closet door. Pearls and pajamas—what a combination! I imagine wearing something fancy. A dark green dress with a low neck and shimmery sleeves, maybe. I'd need something on my ears, though. My hair's too short.

I pick through the rest of the jewelry and find a pair of earrings that have watery purple stones in them. When I put them on, I feel like a different person. I'm not Natalie anymore. Maybe this is how it is to be Kate—or Liz.

I look in the mirror again. I smile big and twirl—like a little girl in a ballet show. Only I never was a little girl who got to learn ballet, was I?

I stop short.

I am Natalie, the monster. I'll never be anyone else.

I take the earrings and pearls off and put the jewelry box back. When I'm finished covering it with sweaters again, I go back to my room and lie on top of the jumbled quilt. I lie there for a long time, writing letters in my head.

Dear Mom,

I'm living with the Parkers now. They're in Heber, which is pretty small, but big enough to get lost in. It's nice to have my own room again.

It's a nice, postcard kind of letter. Short and sweet, so no one worries about you. Maybe that's the kind of letter Mom wants to get, so she can worry about herself and not me. But it's not the kind I want to send her.

I get some paper from my desk and start a second time. My hand hurts from holding the pencil so tightly.

Dear Mom,

Why did you let this happen to me? To us? You could have stopped it. I know you could, if you just tried hard enough. Maybe this is what you wanted. Well, maybe it's what I want, too.

I shake my head. No, it's not what I want.

Dear Mom,

Last time, I tell myself.

Am I ever going to get to come home?

I'm not going to actually send that to her. It sounds too whiny, like a little kid pointing at a balloon in the sky, lost forever.

The truth is, some things just aren't possible. You can't always have what you want. Sometimes you have to be happy with what you have.

And what do I have right now?

I snuggle down into the quilt and wrap memories around me to keep the chill away. Good memories. There are some of those. Right alongside the bad.

One day about a year ago Mom let me climb in bed with her on Sunday morning and we fell asleep together. I woke up before she did, though, and I watched her sleep. Her eyes were purple and swollen and I could see every vein in her face. I mapped them out in my head like they were rivers in a far-away land.

I listened to her breathe next. She'd take these long, deep breaths and let them out slow, and then there'd be a short, shallow one, and another, and then a long one. Sometimes she'd whistle out the long ones like a teakettle ready to burst, or the lone, shrill piccolo in the school band.

She smelled of makeup remover, but she'd missed a spot under her chin, where I could see the difference between the dark orange color she pretended to be and the real pale pink she is. The sheets beneath us were smooth, newly washed on Saturday. The blanket wrinkled underneath her arms and made two cocoon shapes where both our bodies lay side by side. The clock ticked past minute after minute.

The good and the bad, Mom, right there together. For a little while.

chapter
sixteen

Monday I go running with John. When I meet him in the foyer, he looks up at me like he has been expecting me all along, which is irritating.

"You really need better shoes," he says.

I look down and see my right sock hanging out of my sole. "They were fine last time," I say. I figure they'll stay fine for as long as I'm here.

"Cushioning is especially important in the long term," he lectures me. "Without it you could end up with shin splints or a punctured fluid sack below your kneecap."

"Sounds great," I say. "Can we get going? Or are you stalling because you're afraid I'm going to beat you this time?"

John does the paper clip thing, bending straight down to his ankles.

I reach down and try to touch my toes, but I'm about three inches away even when I push myself the hardest.

"Don't bounce," John warns me. "You could tear a muscle that way."

I start to simmer like a pot of Alice's spaghetti sauce. If he pushes too far, I'll boil over too.

"Go down slow and easy, then push yourself farther a bit at a time." He puts his hand on my shoulder to guide me down. "Like that."

I stand back up and shake off his touch. "I'm ready," I say. "How about you?"

It's funny. I can almost see another lecture on his lips, but he stops himself and takes a deep breath instead.

"All right." He opens the door and jogs down the driveway. Jogs, not runs like he did before. I can tell it's for me. If he can't get me to warm up one way, he'll try another.

"Lead foot," I taunt him, and breeze by. I keep ahead down the road to the first turn. Then I hesitate, trying to decide in which direction to go, and he catches up.

"This way," he tells me, picking up the pace.

It rained last night and the roads are still damp, with a few oily rainbows puddled in cracks. The sky is still clouded over.

I like the smell of the wet air, the way it curls my hair up around my ears and eyebrows, where it is longest. Time for a haircut, maybe. Or time to get some barrettes to hold it out of my face while it grows out. I'll have to decide soon.

John takes us out by way of the main road this time, then backtracks a few blocks and runs toward the mountainside. We pass a house I'm sure I've seen before. I think it's one of the ones I passed while I was lost. So we're heading out toward Midway.

"Come up this way. There's a great view." John turns right and we pass a golf course. We're really close to the mountains now.

There's a bunch of construction on the road we're heading down. We hit a sign that says NO THRU TRAFFIC, but John just runs around it.

The road gets worse and worse as we go along. There are a couple houses here and there, mostly farmhouses with sheds attached. I see a cow staring at a big yellow front-end loader like it's trying to figure out what has happened to its world.

Hey, I think, I understand your confusion.

Suddenly, we're at the place where the track team went up. We came at it a different way, but sure enough, there's the place the rabbit family crossed the trail. No sign of them now.

Soon the dirt road gets so muddy our feet are sticking.

"We'll have to try this another time," says John. "It's too wet today."

"Won't hurt my shoes," I say.

Instead of arguing with me, John grins. "You know what Alice will do to us when we get back?" he asks.

"We'll clean off with the hose before we go in," I say. "She'll never know."

John starts up. "I hope there's not a landslide."

I follow behind him. *"Que será, será,"* I say.

Mom used to say it to me when we'd get overdue bill notices. And she was always right. What was coming, came. She couldn't change it and I couldn't, either.

The first hundred yards are bad enough that I think about turning back about every other step. But John's eyes are on me, and he's waiting for me to do just that. That's all I need to keep going. I can't let John win. Not this time.

We hit a switchback and the trail is better for a while, drier, not as steep. I get into a stride, and even the sound of my shoes squishing into the mud is good to me. The damp seeps into my socks, my toes, the bottoms of my feet. It doesn't matter because I'm running. Or trying to.

Two more switchbacks and we're back to the sludge again. My breathing sounds like a car engine that backfires every few feet. I feel like I'm starting again with every step. But I keep going.

I can't help it. I want to go where the track team

went. I want to see what Mary sees when she runs. I want to feel how she feels.

The squirrels hop along in the bushes beside us. They peek out at us like they think we're crazy to be out. Maybe we are.

About a third of the way up, the ground turns red and it's thicker than ever. In a couple places the mud comes up to my ankles. I can't pretend to be running anymore. This is just walking, walking through hell.

"Ready to quit?" John asks when I have to stop before another steep part.

Every breath stabs like a knife. I've got cramps everywhere. The sun is rising in front of us, and if I keep my eyes open for more than a second at a time, they burn.

"Natalie?" John asks again.

I shake my head at him and look back up the trail. I'm going to get there.

I won't stop, John or no John.

"And Alice calls me a masochist," John pants. He's just barely keeping up with me now.

The cracks in the road are getting deeper and harder to cross. I slip and fall into one. The mud drips off my thigh like thick blood.

"Natalie, if we don't head back now, I'm going to be late to work," John says. But it's not a command, just a statement. He's letting me decide. My choice.

I rub some warmth back into my legs and put my hand up to my nose. The mud smells rich, like more money than Mom and I have ever seen.

I'm so close to crying I'm not sure that I haven't already started. My face is dripping, but if I rub at it, I'll just get mud in my eyes.

I go on and on, slipping and pulling myself up. John struggles to keep up. It feels good to beat him, to be better than him at something.

Then I turn a corner and start to slide. I can't stop myself. There's nothing to hold on to. No branches by the road, no rocks that haven't been slimed with mud.

I slip all the way to John, then push him down with me. His head knocks backward as he falls.

"Are you all right?" John asks. His arms are around me and I don't even try to squirm away.

"You're crying," he says. He reaches to wipe away the tears.

I jump up and away from him. "Leave me alone!"

He holds up his hands. "Hey, I was just trying to help."

"Well, I don't need your help."

"Fine," says John. "Your choice." He shakes his head and starts down the hill, leaving me behind.

I feel cold. Isn't this what I wanted, to be left alone? To make my own choices for myself? So why am I still crying?

As I sniffle, I take a long look at the tiny houses below. There is a series of lines connecting them. Roads. Not one of the houses really stands alone. You can't look at one of them without seeing them all.

The runners on the cross-country team have invisible lines connecting them to one another, too.

Maybe there are lines that tie me to John and Alice. To Liz, and even to Kate.

"John, wait!" I call, as loudly as I can.

Way down at the last bend, he turns, his shoulders bowed.

"Wait for me. I want to go back with you."

John stares at me as I come up close to him.

"Look," I say. It's hard to get it out.

John puts up a hand. "You don't have to say anything if you don't want to."

I breathe. The mud feels like liquid ice on my jeans and my skin is breaking out in goose bumps.

"I have to," I say.

"Okay, then." He waits for me.

"You know, I didn't exactly want to come stay with you."

I'm saying it all wrong.

"Yeah," he says, in a low voice.

"But it hasn't been that bad," I get out.

John's face brightens under the mud.

"I'm glad," he says.

I've made him go up this mountain in the mud, ruin his clothes, be late for work. And he can still smile.

"Me too," I say, and I smile back at him.

On the way home, we run in spurts, but not hard. By the time we hit Heber, the sun is up and drying the mud on our shirts. As we get closer to the house, it falls off us in chunks.

John moves automatically to stretch position when we finally reach the driveway.

I watch him, trying to find a word—any word.

He seems to take even longer than usual. Waiting.

"Thanks," I say finally, in a voice like a mouse.

John nods. "You're welcome."

"What in the world—?" Alice shrieks when we walk in. She points at the door. "Out. I'll bring some warm water for you to wash in, but you are not coming into my house looking like that."

John and I shrug at each other, smiling, and walk back out and sit on the steps. We strip off our mud-caked shoes and red-brown socks. Then we shake the mud off of our clothes. Alice brings out water to finish the rest.

"All right, you can come in now," Alice says.

We go in together.

chapter
seventeen

I get to first-period English just after the bell rings. I don't remember about Coach Landers until I look up and see him leaning against Mrs. Sorensen's desk.

He hasn't said a word, just looks around.

He isn't fat, not really. And he doesn't do that comb-over thing with his hair like a lot of balding men do. Whatever hair he has left, he buzzes back to gray fuzz. But what you notice most about his face is his eyes. They're deep set and dark, with bushy gray eyebrows over the top.

"Good morning," he says, not hurrying at all, even though it's already five minutes past the hour.

A couple of kids say "Good morning," too. The loudest is Mary.

"Hmm," says Coach Landers. Then he stares at the boy in the first seat of the row by the door. "Good morning," he says to him.

The boy clears his throat. "Uh, good morning," he mumbles.

"My name is Coach Landers," says the coach.

"I'm—um—my name is James Swensen."

"Nice to meet you, James."

James looks away.

The coach moves on to the next kid in the row, and to the next.

Finally he comes to me.

"Good morning," he says.

"Good morning. I'm Natalie Wills." I figure to get it all done in one breath, so he can move on to whatever comes next.

"How are you today, Natalie?" he asks.

So I'm not going to get off easy. I look at Mary, but she's smiling like it's all just a big joke. This is the man who saved her life? He seems more irritating than heroic.

"I'm fine," I mutter.

"Good. Why do you think it is, Natalie, that we are spending most of today with introductions?"

"I don't know." Why doesn't he ask Mary? I wonder. She probably wants to tell him.

"Why don't you think about it?" he says. "And I'll get back to you." He moves back to his desk, but he doesn't get out the book. He isn't doing anything like teaching English. What kind of a substitute is he?

"So? What do you think?" he asks me again.

I roll my eyes. "I don't know."

"Jeff?" Coach Landers turns and walks over to a boy

across from me, also in the back row. "What do you think? Why are we spending so much time getting to know each other?"

"So you don't forget us?" Jeff blurts out.

Everyone laughs, even Coach Landers. "That's exactly right. So I don't forget you. I don't want to forget any of you." He doesn't say anything after that, just walks up to the desk and sits down at it. His eyes move from student to student, desk to desk. It takes a long time. Pretty soon he's used up the whole period.

The bell rings, and I make a run for the door.

"Natalie!" The coach's voice catches me. I didn't move fast enough.

I turn, expecting him to say something about the track team. He doesn't. "If you ever need someone to talk to"—he hands me a piece of paper with a telephone number on it—"call me. Anytime, day or night. That's my cell phone and I keep it on all the time."

Does he really think I'm going to call him?

"Do you give this to all the kids on your team?" I ask. "Like Mary?"

He shrugs. "She has it," he says.

"And the others?"

"Some do, some don't. I give it to people who seem like they need it. That's all."

It seems like such a strange thing to do, handing

out your cell phone number to random people. But then again, this is the coach who runs with his team and starts English class with a bunch of introductions.

"Did Mary tell you about me?"

"Tell me what about you?" asks the coach.

"Uh—that I'm staying with the Parkers." He and John know each other, right?

"Well, John's a good man." He smiles and his eyes seem to get all but lost in the creases of his face. Small as they are, they are still bright as gold. "I'll bet he has you out running every day then. Good practice for the team."

"It's not practice," I say.

"Oh?"

"No. I'm not joining the team. I just like to run, that's all."

"And why's that?" he asks. His eyes are bigger now, and harder to avoid than ever before.

"Why do I like running?" I babble back at him.

He nods.

"Because—well—" My memory flashes back to the image of the houses all strung together. But I don't even have to say it. He knows.

"It's all about getting connected," he says. "First to the ground. Then to yourself. Then to the rest of the world."

His eyes won't let go of me, and I can't just turn my back on him. I walk out backward, bumping into the door frame. I turn around then.

"See you tomorrow, Natalie," he calls after me.

And I have a sense that he's suddenly become another one of those ties, family or not.

chapter
eighteen

Tuesday night we're all sitting in the living room, watching television. Well, all except for Kate, who can't seem to sit down unless it's "in scene." She's standing by the edge of the screen, watching the lead actress and copying her every move.

"So, what would you like for a birthday breakfast?" Alice asks me.

"Birthday?" Kate's attention is torn away from the screen at last.

"Yes, Natalie will be fourteen tomorrow," says John.

"Fourteen, how special," says Kate in a nasty tone.

John gives her a warning look, and she's quiet for a moment.

"So, Natalie—any requests for the short-order cook?" asks Alice.

I think for a minute.

"Kidney pie? Or kedgeree?" asks Kate in a fake British accent.

I shake my head. "Cold cereal," I decide in the end.

"Cold cereal?" John echoes.

106

"Cold cereal," I say. It's sort of a tradition for me. I've always had cold cereal for breakfast on my birthday.

"You know, I can buy something from the store if you don't want me to cook," Alice tells me. "Muffins. Doughnuts."

"Or Alice can cook her special birthday gruel," adds John.

Kate and Liz giggle.

Alice pokes John in the stomach.

"Ouch. I'm sorry. Terribly, terribly sorry." John laughs.

"Cold cereal is just fine," I say. I wish everyone would stop looking at me. "Really, it's not that big a deal." Please, please stop looking at me.

"All right. Cold cereal it is," says Alice. "But don't think you can get out of cake and ice cream."

I shrug, giving up. I already told them I didn't want a party. I guess cake and ice cream is as little as they can manage to do.

"You like chocolate?" Alice bites at her lip.

"Umm." Is she planning on making it herself? "Chocolate's fine." I can't think of anything easier, and if it's bad, well, it still won't be worse than my usual birthdays.

Kate rolls her eyes and gets up. "Mom, last time you tried to make a cake, you cooked it so long we had to throw the pan out."

Alice holds up her hands. "I'll order it from the bakery. I promise."

"I'll pick it up tomorrow," John says. "Are you sure you want chocolate?" he asks me.

I think about it carefully this time. "Well, maybe lemon," I say, remembering a sample I had once at the bakery up the street from our apartment. "If they have it," I add, feeling selfish. Chocolate is probably everyone else's favorite.

But no one objects. Not even Kate.

John nods. "Lemon it is."

I escape from the living room soon after that and get ready for bed. Running in the mornings makes sleep a lot nicer than it used to be. For one thing, I don't have as many bad dreams.

Tonight, I don't have any at all. My sleep is like a cool, blue lake without a ripple on it. And then the light goes on.

"Happy birthday to you," I hear a chorus of croaky voices sing to me. No one sounds that bad by accident. They have to be trying.

My eyes blink until I can see Kate and Liz standing in their pajamas around my bed. Alice has a housecoat on, the kind with a zipper down the front and big flowers in the wrong color everywhere. John is wearing his sweats.

When the song is over, he hands me two boxes wrapped in silver paper.

I sit up and yawn. The clock says 5:29.

I pull off the ribbon on the smaller box first. Underneath the paper is a shoebox, and inside is a pair of expensive running shoes, the same brand as the ones John ruined on Monday with me.

I run a finger along the clean white leather, then press a finger into the cushion and feel the spring. "Wow," I say. "These are great."

"Well, I had to get myself a new, mud-free pair, so while I was at the store, I got a pair for you, too." John lifts up his sweatpants and shows me his new pair. "Why don't you try them on?"

I push my feet in, then John kneels down next to me and laces them up. "How's that?" he asks.

"They're perfect." They feel like little clouds on my feet.

"Well, if you don't like this kind," John says, "you can always take them back to the store and try on some others. I saved the receipt, just in case."

"Uh—I don't think I'll need it."

John looks like it's his birthday, not mine.

"Open the other one," says Alice, pushing it at me.

This one is from her. I get excited, thinking how great John's present was. Then I see the velour jogging suit in a plummy purple.

What do you say when you get a present you hate? I've never had the experience before. Alice had tried to get something perfect for me. She knew I liked to run, so she must have thought this would be great.

"She hates it," says Kate. "I told you she'd hate it."

"Oh, well," says Alice. "I saved the receipt, too."

"Thanks," I say.

"You ready for breakfast now?" asks Alice.

"We're not going running?" I look at John.

"Not today," he says with a smile.

Then he and Alice head out. Kate and Liz stay.

"Here, we got you this." Liz hands me a small white jewelry box.

Jewelry, for me?

I stare at Kate.

"It's not going to squirt you with ink when you open it, if that's what you're worried about," says Kate.

"Well, with the way you've been acting, there's no reason for her not to expect that," says Liz.

My hands feel numb and clumsy, but I finally open the little box and see a heart-shaped pendant on a tiny gold chain. The pendant has the word *Friend* on it.

I leave it in the box, afraid that if I lift it out, I'll break it.

"Do you like it?" asks Liz.

"Uh . . . ," I say. My throat feels tight. How could I not like it?

"Well, I don't blame you if you don't want to be Kate's friend," says Liz. "But it would be nice if you'd be mine."

"Sure," I say.

"Great," says Liz. She takes the box from my hand

and pulls the necklace out. Her hands are soft as she fastens the chain. The pendant falls just under my nightshirt. "Looks nice, don't you think?" she asks Kate.

"It looks fine," says Kate. "But don't you think you should have asked her before you put it on?"

"And who are you, the queen of courtesy?" asks Liz.

My hand closes around the necklace. I thought Kate hated me. And Liz? I thought she hardly noticed me.

"Anyway, happy birthday," says Liz.

"Yeah, happy birthday," says Kate.

"And—?" Liz prompts Kate.

"And I'm sorry I've been so rude to you."

"Rude and childish," adds Liz.

"Don't push it," says Kate, but she sounds more sad than angry.

"You know you can't blame Natalie for Mom and Dad."

"And who are you, my new therapist?" Kate's head comes up and her eyes flash. She's not acting. She's really mad.

"It's been five years." Liz glances at me and realizes I am clueless.

"Mom lost a baby and got really depressed. She kicked Dad out for a while. That's what started it, anyway. It hit her hard."

"Yeah, and she hit back," says Kate.

"So now you know all our dirt," says Liz. "Welcome to the family." She grins, then nudges Kate.

"I am sorry," Kate says again. And I believe her.

"Breakfast!" John calls from the kitchen.

"Yes, Master." Kate bows in the general direction of the kitchen, back in a role.

"Come on," says Liz. She takes my hand and we walk in together.

My necklace shines in the light of the kitchen chandelier. *Friend.*

I squeeze the pendant tightly, until the word stamps into the flesh of my hand.

The kitchen table has about five boxes of cold cereal on it. Fourteen Cheerios, each with a birthday candle in it, float in my cereal bowl.

There's more "Happy Birthday" singing and then I have to shower for school. I tell myself I should save my new shoes for running, but I can't help it. I have to wear them to school.

The rest of the day is pretty normal. Coach Landers actually teaches us from the book, but it is the no-homework policy that makes everyone like him. I doubt he has the same rule for the cross-country team.

After my last class, I run home from school, trying out my new shoes. It's cold out, but sunny. Nothing to hold me back, nothing to slow me down. I don't take even one wrong turn, and I get home about two minutes before Kate does on the bus.

"How did you do that?" she asks. "You catch a ride with Liz's friend or someone else?"

Yeah, like I know so many people here. "Call it my little secret," I say.

"Oh." Kate puts on a German accent. "Vee haff secrets, do vee?"

"We have secrets," I say.

Kate smiles at me and lets me go.

It's the first halfway normal conversation Kate and I have had. I like it.

In the kitchen, Alice is tying balloons on the chairs around the table. She pops about every other one, but it looks good in the end. There are streamers on the walls and a paper sign that reads HAPPY BIRTHDAY.

"So, what would the birthday girl like for a snack?" Alice asks.

"I'm not really hungry," I say, feeling crowded, and I go to my room.

Sitting at my desk and not doing my homework, I wonder if my mom remembers this is my birthday. No reason to think she will. She's in rehab and probably has lots of things to think about besides me and my birthday.

So why am I even feeling bad?

Dinner is take-out pizza, and finally, it's time for the cake. John puts the box on the table and opens it. It's gorgeous. Yellow roses all over and lacy white frosting on the edges. The only problem is that the writing on the top says HAPPY BIRTHDAY, STEPHANIE.

"I can't believe they did that," John complains.

"I'm sorry, Natalie," says Alice.

"Hey, no big deal," I say. At least I have a cake, right?

"I'll take it back." John starts boxing the cake back up.

Alice looks at the clock. "The store's closed by now."

"Oh." John sits back down. "I could get a new one tomorrow, then," he offers.

"I said it's no big deal." When I'm grown up, I'll make sure no one ever knows it's my birthday. What's the point?

"Here," says Alice. She takes a knife and scrapes off "Stephanie" and cuts in "Natalie." It's not bad. Maybe Alice should try decorating cakes instead of cooking.

Liz puts on fifteen candles. "One for luck," she says and smiles at me.

John lights the candles one by one, until the cake looks like a forest fire, only cheerier. More singing, and Alice nudges me. "Make a wish."

I close my eyes and wish I can have another birthday like this one. But when I try to blow them all out, I miss the last one. The one for luck. Kate gets it for me, trying to sneak in so I don't notice it's her helping. But I do. And wishes don't come true unless you get all the candles yourself.

Alice serves the cake.

"Mmm, good," says Liz at the first bite.

Alice takes a bite, too. "I wonder if I could get their recipe," she says.

No one responds. Everyone else is busy eating the cake. I'm busy picking at mine.

"Something wrong?" Kate asks me.

"No, no," I say. "Everything's fine. You've been great to me. I've never had a birthday like this before. The shoes. The necklace. The cake. The—the—"

"Purple velour jogging suit?" Kate's eyebrows go up and she starts to titter.

I wish I could laugh with her.

I hope to dream of Mom that night. Even if it's the nightmare, I don't care. I just want to be with her, see her face, feel her hands on me. But I sleep without dreams until John's alarm wakes me up at 5:30. I pull myself out of bed to go run with him.

He's there. And she's not.

chapter
nineteen

Two days later, in the mail, there's something for me, no return address listed. My hands shake when Alice offers it to me.

It can't be from my mom. Ms. Beck asked me if I wanted to hear from her and I told her I didn't know. She can't give Mom my address here without getting my permission first, right?

But I certainly recognize the handwriting. The long *e*s that look like *l*s, the way all the letters are smashed together. It's Mom's all right. She must have found a way around the rules.

"You want to go in your room to open that?" Alice asks.

I wonder how she does that. Knows things without anyone telling her, that is.

"Thanks," I say. It's amazing I don't fall down on the way. I can't see anything but the envelope in front of me.

My fingers won't work right and I end up tearing

the card inside the envelope, too. I put it back together with some tape from the bottom desk drawer. Then I stare at the picture of a mother and a baby at a park. Inside, the card reads, "You never forget your first birthday," which seems kind of stupid to me. Everyone forgets their first birthday, don't they?

Unless it comes later. Like when you're fourteen.

Mom's handwriting is scrawled in tiny letters in the corner: "Happy Birthday, Natty. I hope we can spend next year's together—at the park?"

It's a nice thought, right? And Mom actually remembered my birthday. Two good things.

So why am I churned up inside?

I get up and tighten the laces on my shoes, then head out running.

I run about four blocks and turn back. I can't stand it. I have to do something about the card, and running doesn't help.

"What's up?" Alice asks when I come back in. "Your shoes bothering you?"

"Huh?" I look down. "Oh. No, they're fine."

I go back into my room and pick up the card, turning it over and over in my hands. I don't need to open it again to see Mom's words. It's like they're written on my forehead. I can feel them.

Hope we can spend next year's together—at the park?

She remembers spending time with me at Liberty Park. Did it make her happy, too?

She writes these nice things; she probably believes them. But she'll still hurt me again.

I put the card back in the envelope and put it in the bottom drawer of my desk. Then I take out a piece of paper and write another letter to Mom.

I don't write "Dear Mom," like I did with the other letters. I just start right in.

You always say you love me, Mom, but you never show it. Words can't hold me and words can't wipe away my tears. Words can't make me feel safe and loved. Only you can do that.

Every time I see you I wonder when it's going to go bad again, Mom. I wonder when I'm going to hate you again. And the problem is, you've made me start to think the same thing about other people. That they'll let me down eventually. So I haven't even trusted anyone long enough to find out if it's true or not. That's because of you, Mom.

So don't take me to the park next year, Mom. I'll go by myself, or I'll find someone else. Someone who won't let me down.

My legs are cramping from not warming up, but it's my stomach that hurts worse.

I put the letter in the drawer with the card, wishing I had Mom's address so I could send it to her right now. If I wait to ask Ms. Beck for it the next time I see her, I might start to feel sorry for Mom.

I might never send it.

"Hey, Natalie!" Kate pounds on my door.

"What?" My voice is as tired as if I'd run up the mountain in the mud again.

"I was wondering if you wanted to take your jogging suit back today. You know, get something you really want. Mom says she'll drive me to the mall in Provo if you'll come, too. What do you say?"

"I guess so." It's not like I have anything better to do. And if Alice is already planning on taking Kate, then why not?

"Great." She turns around to yell at Alice. "Mom, Natalie says she wants to go right now."

Upstairs at the new Nordstrom, I find a good pair of black sweats that fit, but they're not nearly as expensive as the velour jogging suit.

"Why don't you look around and find something else to make up the difference?" Kate suggests. "Maybe a dress."

A dress? I haven't worn one of those since I was three years old and Mom bought me one so she could take a picture of me to put on the wall. I don't know where that picture is now.

Kate takes me to the dress section. There are shimmery satin ones and lacy ones and ones with velvet on the sleeves. Kate picks out one for herself, and then another. She talks Alice into buying them.

She didn't have completely unselfish motives in wanting to take me shopping, but I don't mind.

I don't like any of the dresses. Whenever I try one on and look in the mirror, I feel like I'm looking into the plastic face of a doll, frozen into a big smile.

"Well, maybe you could take a gift certificate and decide what you want later. That would be one way to make sure we get to come back to the mall."

Yuck. Kate must like shopping a lot more than I do.

"I have another idea," I say. I go over to the boys' jeans section and pick out a pair that looks like they'll fit me. "Let's get these."

"You don't want to try them on?"

I shrug.

"They're close enough," I say, holding the jeans up to my waist. They're almost exactly like the pair I already have, which are nearly worn out. These will last another year or so. Until I'm back with Mom.

I wish I knew if that was going to be a good thing or not. I don't even know what to hope for. For her to flop out fast, before I get used to having her around. Or for one last chance to spend time with her, before I get taken away forever.

chapter
twenty

"Hey, Natalie!"

I'm standing in front of my locker, waiting for the after-school crowd to die down, and hear Mary's voice behind me.

I turn.

"I was wondering . . ."

I slam the locker shut and she jumps.

She recovers quickly, though. "There's a track meet on Saturday. I thought you might like to come run." She hands a flyer to me so fast I don't have any time to tell her I'm not coming.

"That's directions to the meet," she says. "And anything else you need to know if you're planning to come. I told Coach Landers I'd give them to you. Just in case you're ready to give the team a try."

Hmm. Why didn't he give them to me himself? He didn't seem the shy type.

"Well," says Mary, "see you. I hope."

"You have practice today?" I ask.

But she shakes her head. "No practice before a meet.

We have to rest up so we can really kill ourselves." She smiles like she's looking forward to it. Then she heads off.

I stuff the paper into my back pocket and shoulder the backpack. I walk out of the school.

The buses are gone and the football team hasn't come out onto the field yet. There's no one here, really, but me. I like it that way.

When I reach the edge of the school property, I roll my shoulders and get ready for the run home. I do a few easy jogs as I cross the street, then get up to full speed in the first block. The sun's beating down on my hair, making me glad I don't have it any longer than it is.

"I'm not going to that track meet," I tell myself out loud.

So why do I keep the paper in my pocket? Why didn't I throw it away at school?

The rest of the way home I go easy, jogging more than running. My shoulders hurt from the backpack and I haven't broken in my new shoes yet. There's one spot on my right foot, and the beginning of my pinkie toe, that rubs hard on the side. And the more I think about it, the more I hurt.

I'm a big baby. I walk up the porch steps. I'd never make it on the team. Mary would be out in the lead, but I'd be hopping behind on one foot, trying to save my pinkie toe a little pain.

When I get to my room, I take off my shoes and

look at my right foot. No blood. It's hardly red at all. Once the shoe is off, it feels just fine again.

I put it up anyway, wiggle it so that it feels some air. Then I relax until dinner.

"How was school today?" John's usual question at the table.

"Fine." My usual answer.

Tonight is Mexican night. Hard-shell tacos—Alice doesn't have to cook those. Or burn them, rather. Hamburger for the inside, but if you put on enough salsa, you can't taste anything else. It's a good strategy with Alice's food.

On my second taco, I take a big crunching bite and everything falls apart, right in my lap.

"Oh, hurry, get that off," says Alice. "Tomato is a terrible stain."

I'm wearing my new jeans, so I actually care about staining them. I change into my sweats in my room, then come out and hand the pants to Alice. I remember about the flyer in the back pocket too late.

"Here," says Alice, handing it to me right in front of John. "You don't want to wash this."

I crumple up the paper and try to think of where I can put it. But sweats have no pockets, and I end up playing with it in my hands.

"What's that?" John asks.

"Nothing," I say.

But John can't let it go at that. He leans forward and catches a glimpse of the title. "Hey, that's for the cross-country meet on Saturday. Are you planning to go to it?"

"Well." I stumble over the words. "There's this girl, Mary. She's in one of my classes and she's on the team, too. She asked me to come." I'd go watch her. That's all. Just watch.

"Great," says John. "We'll go together."

"Okay," I say. Then I sit back down and finish eating.

John pulls me aside before I head back to my room. "You're sure? I don't want to push you into it if you weren't planning on going."

"Mary wants me to," I say.

John nods. "And she's your friend."

She's as much a friend as I have.

"So, anyone else want to come?" John asks, walking back to the kitchen.

"I'm coming. I'll just bring a book or something to keep me busy," Liz says.

"Count me in, too," says Kate.

John gasps loudly. "You? At a sports event?"

Kate shrugs. "It won't be that bad, if Natalie's there. Besides, I don't have anything else to do."

So it was all decided. We'd go.

chapter
twenty-one

John drives us all to the track meet in the white sedan. Alice is in front with him. I sit in back and listen to Liz talk about her new debate partner. Kate makes faces just behind Liz, so she can't see.

It's hard not to laugh out loud. I forget that I should be nervous until John says, "Here we are."

"Here" is in Park City, by some ski jumps without any skiers on them. Instead there are about a hundred boys and half as many girls. Mary stands out from all of them somehow. There are a couple of girls taller than her, but she's the one who looks most confident. Even standing still, she looks fast.

She waves at me and motions for me to come over. "Oh, good. You're wearing your running shoes," she says, looking down at my feet.

"Uh . . . ," I say. "I thought I'd just watch."

I crane my neck around, but I can't see any bleachers.

Mary shrugs. "Well, it's up to you, but there's not that much to watch at a cross-country meet. You run along the cones, and when you hit the finish line, you're done."

"But—" I'm not ready for this. I'm really not.

"You didn't go running already this morning, did you?" she asks.

"No."

"Then you're ready." Mary acts like it's all settled.

How does she know if I'm ready or not? I look at John.

"I think you should go for it," he says.

I breathe in. I realize I feel good. Maybe too good.

"You'll do great," says Mary. She's bending down doing stretches just like the ones John does every morning. She could probably fold herself into a desk drawer if she wanted to.

"Yeah, right." First time and I'll win. Sure, that's the way it goes. I bend over and do a few stretches, making me look good.

Kate comes up. "So, where are we going to wait for them to come in?"

"Down the road about three miles that way." Mary points.

I have the perfect chance to get rid of Mary and to avoid the meet. If I really want to, I can just go with Kate and Liz. But I don't want to.

"You go on with Alice and Kate and Liz," I tell John.

His eyes get big.

"Well then, good luck," says John, and waves good-bye. He and the others get back in the car and drive away.

Mary's head comes down to her ankles. She's breathing more deeply.

There's no going back now.

Coach Landers comes over. He's wearing sweatpants and a T-shirt that lets his stomach poke out at the bottom. "So, you came," he says.

"Yeah."

"Good to have you here." He pats me on the shoulder. "You know you're not official yet."

"I know."

"It'll be a trial run this time. If you like it, we'll sign you up. Then you can run as part of the team."

"Thanks," I say.

He nods and drifts off.

"Come on. Stretch," says Mary, her face all the way in the dirt now.

I lean down and follow her moves, thinking all the while about the miles ahead of me. Will I be last? Will I embarrass everyone?

I should be burning, the way Mary is making me hold, hold, hold. I thought John was bad about warming up, but Mary is worse. Funny that I feel so cold.

"It's only about three miles," Mary says. She stands up and swings her arms, slowly at first, then faster.

Big circles, little circles. Then across her chest. And reaching behind her back.

Three miles. Suddenly, I don't know if I can manage three steps.

"Time to line up," says Mary, waving me to come with her.

Coach Landers is walking around, finding everyone on the team, and giving last-minute advice.

"Don't let yourself get too far behind at first," he tells Mary.

Then he turns to me. I start to shake.

"Think about the dirt. Connect with it," he says. He bends down and grabs a handful, then lifts it to my nose.

I breathe in the smell and I feel a tightness in my chest start to loosen up. Then I look around at the golden mountains topped with silver-blue sky. I feel the connection, for just a second. I want to feel it again.

A shot rings out and all the other girls surge ahead.

It's started. I've started. My legs are moving.

Mary is right next to me.

"Coach said you weren't supposed to stay too far behind," I say.

Mary shrugs. "I'll catch them."

"Listen, you don't have to stay with me. I'll be fine."

But Mary only shakes her head. "I'm not worried about it. You shouldn't be, either."

I pick up the pace a bit and Mary keeps up easily. The connection is coming back. I feel like I could run a marathon.

I speed up again.

"Keep it slow your first time," Mary says, right at my side.

I slow down a fraction as we start up a hill. I remember when I first saw Mary running, going up the hill with Coach Landers and all the boys.

"Do the boys run a different race?" I ask.

"Yeah. Five or six miles, usually."

"You're not allowed to run with them?" I bet she could.

"Not this year," she says, with a smile. "But Coach says he might try to get me permission later. If I need more competition to train for college."

We head down now, and Mary lets me go faster. The path is marked with orange cones and is part asphalt, part dirt. My pinkie toe aches, but I hardly notice it. The new shoes are definitely going to be broken in after this.

We catch up to a big group of runners clumped together in twos and threes.

"Hey, Mary," says one of them.

She waves and we move past like we're on a train and they're all watching.

It doesn't faze me at all. Running with Mary is

even better than running alone. It's not so much about getting away from someplace. It's not even about getting to someplace.

It's about enjoying the way.

We've run a mile or more already. So we're almost halfway done and I don't feel the pain yet at all.

Mary puts on the steam as we head out across a long straight stretch. I keep up with her every step of the way. Right at the end of my vision, I can see a few of the best runners stretched out in a line, like they're on a track, jostling for position.

We hit a slight incline, but Mary's like a steamroller. I'd be letting myself ease back by now, if I were running alone, but I don't want to lose her, so I have to push it. I keep hoping for a second wind, but so far, I haven't hit it.

We're tagging the last of the top runners. She's got long blond hair in a ponytail down her back and she's very thin. But she doesn't have Mary's muscles.

She nods as we go past.

I'm still up with Mary. I can't believe it. And she's not losing. I was sure I'd slow her down. Either that or she'd have to leave me behind.

My breath burns in my chest and I'm a bit lightheaded. It doesn't feel so good now, except for the wind in my face. Then I realize there isn't any wind. It's me.

We go by Sandra, Michelle, Jenna, and Aubrey. Mary knows all their names, and they know her, too. None of them seems mad she's passing them. In fact, they look like they expect it, and they all say hello to me.

I don't have the energy to be nervous about them now.

Suddenly I get a cramp in my leg and start flagging. Mary slows down with me. The other runners are pounding behind us, eager to take her place up front.

"Go on, Mary. Don't wait for me."

She ignores me. "You just have to run through it," she says. "That's the only way to get the pain to go away."

I limp along and Aubrey passes us.

I try to push myself to go faster, but I want to stop. The cramp is not just in my leg anymore. It's everywhere.

"It will only hurt more if you stop right now," says Mary. "Believe me, I know."

"Go ahead." I'm angry with her now. "Go on without me."

"Hey, I'm your friend," says Mary. "I'm trying to help."

"Who—said—you—were—my—friend?" I ask. Oh, I'm panting heavily and I feel worse than ever.

Jenna and Michelle go by us.

The finish line is in the distance. There's no way we can win now.

"I am your friend," says Mary. And she won't go ahead.

Suddenly I feel a surge of new energy. My breath is coming easier, and my legs kick up behind me.

Mary and I breeze forward.

Then we're into a full sprint. There are faces ahead of us, at the finish line. Coach Landers, shouting something with his hands around his mouth. John, waving excitedly. Alice jumping—well, bouncing up and down. Even Kate and Liz are watching for me.

I'm drowning in sweat, but Mary is still next to me. I keep pushing and pushing.

We pass more runners. I'm going to give it my best, so Mary knows what that is. So I know, too.

Then we've hit the tape together and I hear a roar of sound. Is it just in my ears or is that the crowd?

"You did it!" Mary holds my hand.

It has about as much life in it as a fish stick.

"We did it," I say. I couldn't have done it without her, but that takes nothing from me. If anything, it makes it better.

John appears in front of me, and Alice's arms stretch around me. Soft.

"Here, drink this." Kate's voice, and then there's a bottle under my nose.

I open my mouth. Kate gets the idea, and dribbles the water in for me. It tingles, like champagne. But it's only water. I know it is.

"You won," says Liz. "You really won."

I really won. And it feels like it was more than just a race.

chapter twenty-two

Ms. Beck comes in November for her first month's visit.

"You're looking good, Natalie," she tells me.

I blush a little. I've been putting more weight on my arms and legs, which I probably needed.

"You feel like you're adjusting?" Ms. Beck asks. She's got her hair up in the bun, as usual, and she's wearing her blue suit with the flower pin in the lapel. Ugh.

"Yeah, pretty well."

"School records say you're doing fine there."

I am doing better than I'd expected, actually, considering how little time I spend on homework. I even got a B in my math class, after I let John help me study for the last test.

"How about your foster sisters? Do you get along with them?"

"Liz and Kate? Yeah." I'm surprised there, too. The way things went the first week, I was worried I'd wake up one morning and find myself sleeping in glue. Or something worse.

"And Mr. and Mrs. Parker?"

"I run with John sometimes. Sometimes with Mary, a girl from school."

Ms. Beck scratches at an ear and a couple of hairs from her tight bun fall out. It actually looks better that way. I keep quiet about it, though. If she knew, she'd probably excuse herself to go into the bathroom and tuck them back up.

"So you're making friends. That's good."

"She's on the cross-country team," I say.

"Well, are you thinking of joining?"

"Thinking," I say. But no commitment. Not yet.

"So you really like running?" she asks.

"It feels good," I say. "It takes my mind off other things."

"Ah," says Ms. Beck, like she understands everything now. "Anything else you want to tell me?"

Anything else? Isn't she going to say something about my mom?

"There is one last thing I wanted to talk to you about," she says.

My heart jumps into my throat. I open my mouth, but a croak is all that comes out.

"Have you thought about seeing your mother? Or talking to her on the phone, at least? I talked to her last week and she's very anxious about you."

"She is?"

"Yes. She's doing very well in rehab," Ms. Beck

goes on. "She says it's the thought of getting you back that keeps her going through all the hard stuff."

I think about Mom's birthday card. John gave me new running shoes, which Mom never could have. Alice bought me the purple velour jogging suit. Kate and Liz gave me the friend necklace, which I never take off.

But it's the card that's most precious to me. The first birthday card Mom has ever given me.

"Her counselor expects her to check out in another two or three months. She plans to reapply for your custody then."

"What?" My eyes are spinning and I feel sick to my stomach.

Am I running a race backwards? It's hard to keep going when I don't know for sure if I want to get to the finish line or not.

"Actually, she'll have to wait to apply for custody until a few months after her release, once she proves herself capable of taking on more responsibility." Ms. Beck sounds like a TV weatherperson. Sixty percent chance of rain next Friday. Better bring an umbrella to school. Only what kind of umbrella works on Mom's kind of rain?

"What if I don't want to go?" I say.

"Well, the judge will certainly give you a chance to air your opinion at the hearing," says Ms. Beck.

"But if the judge says I have to go back, then I have to, right?" I'm just trying to think ahead.

"You'd rather stay with the Parkers?" asks Ms. Beck. "I didn't think you'd become so attached to them." She gets out her notebook again and scribbles for a few seconds.

"Wait! I didn't mean that. I do want to go back with Mom." My ears go red, and I'm sure Ms. Beck sees them. She's probably writing that down, too. "It's just that I don't—I mean, I'm not sure—"

"You don't trust your mother, is that it? That's normal, under the circumstances."

I look out the window and notice it is getting dark all of a sudden. In Heber you don't have such a good view of incoming clouds as you do in other places. The wind blows a storm into the canyon, and then it's there. Whether you like it or not.

"You know, Natalie, I—"

I turn and catch her eyes, cloudy and uncertain. Then she looks down again. What was she going to say?

"Well, I'll keep you posted on your mother. Is that what you'd like?"

"Yes." That is one thing I am sure of.

Ms. Beck puts the notebook in her bag, then walks into the kitchen to talk to Alice.

The rain on the window beats down like hundreds of tiny feet on pavement. More than a team of runners, a whole horde of them. I've already been running this morning with John. Just thinking about it makes my legs ache. I bend down to stretch them out. When I stand up again, I see my reflection in the window and start.

I look just like my mom. How did that happen? And when? She has the same dark, fine hair. And her eyes—her eyes are purply-blue like mine, with the same teardrop shape. Thin pink lips, a jaw that quivers like a leaf.

I turn away from the image. The rain has slowed now.

"You all right, Natalie?" Alice asks when I come into the kitchen.

"Yeah," I say quietly.

"Dinner will be ready soon." Ms. Beck is packing up her things and shaking her raincoat on over her bony shoulders.

"Thank you again, Mrs. Parker," says Ms. Beck. "And thank you, too, Natalie. For being willing to try again."

I walk out with her.

"Is there anything else?" she asks me.

"I—uh—" My tongue flops around. "About my mom," I finally get out.

"Yes?" She has that intense look again.

I can't stand it. "Never mind," I say.

But she won't let it go at that. "It's all right, Natalie. Take your time." She waits.

I'd rather run twenty miles up the back of Mount Timpanogos. But there's no getting out of this. So here goes. "You said she wants to see me."

A nod.

"Okay."

"Okay that she wants to, or okay that you want to, too?" Ms. Beck asks.

"Uh-huh," I say.

"Which one?"

She wants me to say it all over again?

"I want to see her."

"Wonderful." She beams. "That's great news, Natalie. Really great. I'll tell your mother." She reaches for the door.

"But—when?" I ask.

"As soon as I can, Natalie. I'll call you, okay?"

"Thank you," I say.

She smiles, showing crooked teeth. Maybe that's why she hasn't smiled much before. Maybe she's one of those people who never got braces as a kid. Maybe she had a mom who couldn't afford it and that's why she became a social worker.

It's something to think about. I could be a social worker someday, too. Maybe.

"You're welcome, Natalie. You're very welcome." Her mouth closes over her teeth. Then she waves at me and goes out into the rain.

chapter
twenty-three

The day before my meeting with my mom, Liz slips into my room.

"Hi." She leans against my desk and looks at everything in the room except for me.

I wonder what we're waiting for. Then Kate comes in, too.

"Hi," she says. Her hair is in braids today, for a part she is doing at school. She's got a fake black mole on one of her cheeks and lipstick smeared across her face. She looks funny, but I've never seen her so serious before.

"So?" I say.

Kate looks at Liz. Liz looks at Kate. "Uh—" they say at the same time. Then they bite their lips and go quiet.

Quiet with Kate and Liz. Definitely serious.

"We came—" Kate says in one of her fake accents.

Liz jabs her in the side. "Don't do that."

Kate moves over to the door. She flips the light switch on and off like a strobe light.

I cover my eyes and wave at her to stop.

"Whoops," she says. "I guess we can be pretty annoying. Even when we're not trying to be."

"We came to wish you luck," Liz says.

"For tomorrow," Kate finishes. "With your mom."

"Oh," I say.

"Is there anything we can do to help?" asks Kate.

"You look scared to death," says Liz.

Gee, thanks. Just what I wanted to hear.

"I'll come with you if you want," says Kate.

"No!" I say.

Kate looks miserable. "Yeah. Dumb question," she says.

"Dumb questioner," says Liz.

"No," I say. "That's not what I meant. I really appreciate the offer, but I just . . ." Funny how many times I wished I could be by myself and Kate and Liz were there anyway. Or John and Alice. Or Mary and Coach Landers.

Now I wish someone could go with me, and I know they can't.

"She's my mom," I say. The words ring loudly in my own ears.

"So you have to love her, right? No matter how bad she is," says Kate.

"Well," I say, "I guess I don't have to. I could hate her."

"But you don't," says Liz. "Do you?"

There's a long silence then.

"No," I say.

The front door opens and Alice calls out for everyone to come help bring in the groceries. I go, too. I don't like bringing in the groceries, but it means I'm part of the family.

It means I belong.

chapter
twenty-four

Ms. Beck pulls into the driveway the next day in her bright red truck. I've seen it before, but it's always a bit of a shock. It just doesn't seem to fit her at all.

I'm waiting in the foyer, but I let her ring the doorbell anyway.

"You look just like your mother," she tells me.

"Yeah?" Is there some way I can still change my mind? I'm so scared I can't even shake.

"You're both terrified of getting hurt again," says Ms. Beck.

Well, she's got that right. "Let's go," I say, because there's no point in waiting around at the starting line while the race is being run ahead of you. Might as well get going.

From the high truck cab, I look back at John and Alice's house. It seems smaller and bigger than when I first came. Smaller because I know it all, and bigger because of everything that happened there.

I tell myself not to cry, but the tears are falling as soon as I turn my back on the house. John isn't home yet, and Kate and Liz are shopping at the mall with some friends. They offered to stay, but I told them I didn't want a send-off. It's not like I won't be back. At least for a while.

"So," says Ms. Beck. We're on the highway that winds up to Park City. There are a few other cars on it, but it's too early for evening traffic yet. "What should we talk about?"

"I don't know."

"Not your mom, I'm guessing."

I give her a pleading look.

"You ever think about your dad?"

That hardly seems better. "Never knew him," I say.

"I know. Me, either. But that doesn't keep me from thinking about him."

"Really?" It's the first time she's said anything personal.

She nods. "Left my mom when he found out she was pregnant. Never sent a dime to help her. Us." She twists at a ring on her right hand. Maybe it was her mom's.

"I hated my stepfather for a long time. Told myself all these stories about my real dad. He would have done everything right."

"You think so?" My dad never even saw me. A guy like that would have to be a jerk, right? Even worse than Mom.

Ms. Beck lets out a big sigh. "Not really. I guess I was just pretending because it hurt less that way."

"Hmm," I say.

"Really, things started to get better once my mom married my stepfather. We didn't move around so much and we had a little money. But that's when I started running away."

"You?" I have a hard time believing it.

"Yes, me. I ran away five times between the ages of twelve and fifteen."

"Wow."

"The last time my mom said she wouldn't take me back if I did it again."

Ms. Beck has to concentrate on her driving after that.

"You mind if I roll down the windows?" Ms. Beck asks.

"Fine," I say.

The wind blows Ms. Beck's hair out of her bun strand by strand. At first she tries to pin it back up, one-handed. Then she gives up altogether and takes out the pins.

I've never seen her with her hair all the way down before. She looks even younger than I thought she was.

"And before you ask," she says, "I'm twenty-five. And I've been working as a licensed social worker for three years."

"I wasn't going to—" I say.

"But you wanted to," she says. "Why do you think I keep my hair up all the time? People think of me as too young to do my job."

Maybe she's right.

"Now do you want me to keep talking or would you rather distract yourself some other way?"

Is that what she was doing? "How about we just listen to the radio?"

Ms. Beck thinks about it for a minute, then runs a hand through her hair. "Turn it on," she says. "But don't tell anyone, okay? You'll ruin my image."

"I won't," I promise. And for the rest of the drive, I lean back in my seat and let the music play over me. It feels like I'm letting my hair down, too.

"Here we are," sings Ms. Beck along with the song. Then she turns it off.

I look up and see the old group home. The gray stucco on the front might as well be cement. Suddenly the day feels rainy gray, even though the sun is bright.

Ms. Beck sweeps her hair back up into the bun and sticks the pins in on either side. "Does this look all right?" There's a little tuft on one side and I debate not telling her, just so everyone else can see her with freaky hair. But if she found out, she'd never trust me again.

"Right there," I say, pointing to the left side.

"Oh, thanks." She sweeps it up again, then pins it perfectly. Finally she smoothes down her skirt and opens the door.

She has to wait for a minute on the group home steps before I get there. I just can't make myself go any faster. My whole body is prickly with pins and needles.

"Well, here goes." Ms. Beck turns the knob on the door.

I poke my head in after her and look around the front room, where I met John and Alice for the first time. It seems a long time ago.

But Mom's not there.

"She's in the kitchen," Ms. Beck tells me.

I head toward the kitchen.

Mom is sitting in the chair in front, the one that used to be mine. She looks thin and pale.

"Natty." She puts a hand to her throat. "Oh, Natty." She stands up, takes a step toward me, then stops.

"Hi." My legs don't want to move.

Finally Ms. Beck pulls a chair out for me. "Here. Sit."

I do.

There's a long silence after that.

I wish Liz and Kate were here, making noise, yelling at each other about something stupid.

Mom looks up at me. "You're looking so grown up, Natty. It's like I haven't seen you for years."

"Mom?"

"Yes, Natty?" I thought she'd look better after rehab, but she doesn't. She looks worse. She looks old and tired out. Like she's been running for too long and can't take one more step.

"Call me Natalie," I say. "Natty is for gnats."

She blinks once, then nods her head. "All right, Natty. I mean, Natalie."

"Thanks," I say.

"So," says Ms. Beck, "you two want to talk by yourselves for a while?"

"No," I say quickly.

"No," Mom says a shade after me.

"I mean—"

"You can stay," Mom says.

I nod at Ms. Beck. "Please."

Ms. Beck moves over to the far side of the table and takes the seat that used to be Sharon's. Is Sharon still here or is she in a foster home, too? Maybe she's even home with her dad now, if they found him. I hope she's happy, wherever she is. I hope she thinks about me sometimes.

"How are you?" Mom begins.

"Fine," I say.

"Really?" Mom leans forward a little like she's going to take my temperature.

"Well, mostly," I say.

Mom sits back. "What part isn't fine?" she asks.

"You," I say.

Mom sighs. "Yeah. Well, no need to guess there. I guess I've been pretty much the worst mother any kid could ever be cursed with."

There's another long, weird silence.

I'm thinking of Alice.

"Well," I say. "Maybe there are better mothers."

Mom starts to cry softly.

"But," I say, "you're mine."

She cries harder.

"Ms. Wills?" asks Ms. Beck.

Mom shakes her head and sniffles. "Sorry," she says. Then she turns back to me. "Sorry, Natty. Natalie."

I tap my feet on the tile floor.

"I liked the birthday card, though," I say.

"You did?" Mom's mouth shakes. "I was worried you'd be angry. I didn't send it until your birthday, and then I knew it would come too late."

"At least you remembered," I say. "That was the most important thing."

The corners of Mom's mouth turn up. Not quite a smile.

Ms. Beck nods encouragingly.

"Listen, things are going to get better. I promise," says Mom.

"Yeah?"

"Yeah," says Mom.

Even though we're in the group home, it feels like a real home. At least a little bit.

Ms. Beck stands up and I realize for the first time that it is dark outside. "Well, I'm sorry to say this, but it's time for me to take Natalie back."

Mom wipes at her cheeks and then leaves her hands

there to keep them warm. She used to do that all the time when I was a kid. She hasn't done it for so long that I'd forgotten it. She never wore a coat, either, when she did drugs. She never felt the cold then. She doesn't feel anything on drugs.

"See you soon, Natalie," says Mom.

"Yeah."

She hesitates, looks at Ms. Beck, then turns back to me. She leans over and gives me a kiss on the cheek. Her lips are dry, but warm. "I love you," she says.

"I love you, too, Mom." I muffle the words in her shoulder, then step away. "Bye."

"I'll talk to you again next week, Ms. Wills," says Ms. Beck.

Mom nods and I can feel her eyes on me as I walk out.

"That went well, I think," says Ms. Beck as she buckles herself back into the truck. "What do you think, Natalie?"

"I guess," I say.

"You ready?" Ms. Beck asks me.

"Yes." I've never felt more ready.

She backs the truck up and we get back onto the highway.

"I'm going to go home with her again, aren't I?" I ask, blinking my eyes in time with the flash of cars as they drive past us on the other side of the divider.

"I think I'll be recommending that, yes." It's too dark to see her face.

"It'll be weird to leave John and Alice," I say. And Kate and Liz. And Mary and Coach Landers, too. And Heber.

"Maybe you and your mom could talk about moving to Heber," says Ms. Beck.

"You think she would?" I ask. Mom's a city person. She grew up in a small town and hated it. Hated the smell of cows and the land going out and out forever. So she's lived in cities ever since. Los Angeles. Vegas. Salt Lake City.

Big places, where you can get lost.

"Why don't you talk to her about it?" says Ms. Beck. "Sometimes the best way to change your life is to change where you live it."

"Hmm." It would be harder for Mom to find her old friends again. And harder for them to find her. You can probably get drugs anywhere, even in Heber. But if it takes more effort, maybe Mom would have time to get stronger.

Ms. Beck leans over and switches the radio on. "If you don't mind, that is?" she asks me.

"No, I don't mind." But I don't really hear it on the way back through the canyon up into the mountains and down again.

"We're almost there," Ms. Beck warns me when we hit the HEBER sign at the city limits. I can't believe how familiar everything seems. I can't imagine getting lost here ever again.

"Here you go." Ms. Beck leaves the engine idling this time, but turns on the light. Her hair is down again. I like it that way. "Call me if you need anything, Natalie, will you?"

"Sure." I've got her phone number somewhere in my things. "And thanks for driving me all that way, Ms. Beck. I appreciate it."

"Eugenie," she says.

"Huh?"

"My name is Eugenie," she says. She blushes in the car light. It makes her look younger than ever.

"I guess I can see why you make everyone call you Ms. Beck, then."

"Ha," she says.

I reach for the door.

"Oh, and Natalie." She calls me back. "It was good the last time. When I went back to my mom."

"It was?"

She nods. "I spent six years with her before she died of a heart attack. I wouldn't have missed those years for anything."

I can't seem to make my throat work after that, so I hop out. Once I'm inside the house again, I wave.

chapter twenty-five

Alice and John are waiting up for me in the living room. Kate and Liz are there, too, talking over the television.

"You must be exhausted," says Alice. "Let me get you something to eat."

I'm suddenly starving, enough that I don't care that Alice is cooking.

In the kitchen, she gives me a plate of burritos.

"Really good," I say, my mouth full.

"I told her that, too," John says, and pinches Alice's cheek. "But maybe if a fourth person agrees, she'll start to believe us."

"So." Kate jumps in where Alice and John hadn't dared. "How'd it go?"

"Good," I say, and take another bite. "Good."

"Is that it?" asks Kate. "Just good?"

"Good," I say again.

"Hey, good's good enough for me," says John.

Kate groans and punches him in the arm. Then she looks at me. "It's good to have you home."

"Hey," says Liz. "That was supposed to be my line."

"Time for bed, you two." John puts his hands on their shoulders and steers them out of the kitchen. "You've got school tomorrow.

"You want to talk about it?" John asks when he comes back.

I pick up a few stray pieces of lettuce with my fingertips, then pop them into my mouth. "Not really," I say.

Alice nods and takes my plate away. Her slippered feet shuffle across the kitchen floor.

"Come running with me tomorrow?" asks John.

I take a breath. "Yeah," I say. "I'd like that." I don't know how many more chances I'll have to do it, but I'll take them while they come. Maybe I'll even join the team. Cross-country season is over, but I could do track. With Mary.

"Better be heading to bed, then." John yawns, which makes me yawn, and then Alice starts yawning, too.

John walks me to my room. "Good night," he says.

"Good night." He closes the door and I snuggle underneath the thick quilt. I measure the shadows in the room. Dresser, window, closet, door. They feel like they're mine now.

chapter
twenty-six

I'm in the laboratory again. The vials and tubes are all in alphabetical order up on the shelf. I'm sitting on the table, but there aren't any straps on it this time.

"Natalie," Mom says. She's standing right next to me now, holding my hand. "Are you ready?"

"Ready for what?"

She puts a finger to her lips and then goes to open the door.

In come Kate and Liz and John and Alice, all wearing white lab coats. Kate has funny glasses with a fake mustache. Liz's mouth is opening and closing nonstop, even though I can't hear what she's saying. John is sweating a storm down his face, and he stops in the doorway to do his cool-down. Alice comes in with a tray of pancakes.

"For you," she says.

I give them to Mom, who takes a bite and tries not to make a face.

Then Mary runs in with Coach Landers close behind.

"You," says Coach Landers to me.

"What?"

He points to the door. The whole track team is out there, waiting for me. I look down and see that my running shoes are already on my feet. I'm wearing the purple velour jogging suit, too. I can't seem to get rid of it, even in my dreams.

"Run," says Mary, taking my hand.

And I run.